What goes on the title ┃

The title, the autho

MW00736618

PUBLISHING BASICS

A Guide for the Small Press and Independent Self-Publisher

Robert Bowie Johnson, Jr.

with

Ron Pramschufer

RJ Communications LLC, New York
In cooperation with
Solving Light Books Annapolis, Maryland

Where does the copyright page appear, and what's on it?

The copyright page is usually found on the back of the title page. We have the copyright notice, which includes the word "copyright," the symbol ©, the year, and the authors' names. You don't need both the word "copyright" and the symbol. Either will do, but just about every publisher uses both.

We have the publisher's name and address. We have the Library of Congress Catalog Number (LCCN), which is not required, and the International Standard Book Number (ISBN). We tell you where this book was printed. It is always a good idea to give credit to the printer and the designer as well.

Library of Congress Catalog Number: 00-190819
ISBN 10: 0-9700741-4-X
ISBN 13: 978-0-9700741-4-0

Published by RJ Communications LLC, New York
In cooperation with Solving Light Books, Annapolis, MD

Design and layout by SelfPublishing.com

Printed in the United States of America

This is a  book.

How is this book organized to help me understand the self publishing process?

We answer the most frequently asked questions (FAQs) about self publishing and we steer you in the right direction. If, after reading this book, you have additional questions, please submit them directly through the *SelfPublishing.com* Web site.

Five different kinds of paper and three different printing processes are used in this book. They are:

- 50# white offset (512ppi), printed offset
- 50# natural offset (400ppi), printed offset
- 45# Alternative Offset (400ppi), printed offset
- 60# recycled offset (434ppi), printed digitally
- 60# white offset (444ppi), printed digitally

The first 128 pages of this book are printed on a web offset press, and the last 8 pages are on digital presses.

The same photographs and artwork are printed in each section so that you can compare the quality of the reproduction for the various printing methods.

Now and then we drop in a vivifying touch of humor to make sure that a stale groove doesn't trap the spinning wheels of your creative mind. Publishing your own books should be exciting and fun!

CONTENTS

Is this the Acknowledgments page?

Yes, it is. While you are writing your books, keep a special folder or electronic file to make note of the people and organizations that help you. If you don't do this, you will most likely forget some very important people. You can't go wrong giving credit where credit is due. The people who help you write your books are your allies in the books' promotion.

I want to thank everyone who has asked me a question about self publishing, and all those who have helped me frame the answers to those questions.

Is this the Dedication page?

Yes, and I dedicate this work to the memory of Erwin Knoll (July 17, 1931–November 2, 1994), former editor of *The Progressive* magazine, who taught me how to write and inspired me to be a writer. Teachers such as he are rare.

Publisher's Note to the Third Edition

The year 2000 marked the initial printing of *Publishing Basics: A Guide for the Small Press and Independent Self-Publisher.* Over 20,000 copies have been distributed to a variety of writers, poets, and publishers. Since that date, RJ Communications, through its various Web sites, including *SelfPublishing.com* and *BooksJustBooks.com*, has overseen the printing of over 105 million books and helped thousands of individuals and companies reach their publishing goals. This third edition of *Publishing Basics* is an updated version that has been updated to keep pace with the many changes that have occurred since 2000 and also includes many questions not answered in the first two editions. Many of the new questions and answers are taken from my "Ask Ron" column in the *Publishing Basics* Newsletter and Web site. I would highly recommend anyone reading this to subscribe to the *Publishing Basics* Newsletter by visiting *PublishingBasics.com*. Also, since the last edition of the book, the *Publishing Basics* weekly Podcast was launched at *WBJBRadio.com*, where weekly we help you navigate the self publishing minefield. (For you editor types, we have purposely spelled "self publishing" without the hyphen throughout this book to correspond with our Web site.) I hope that you enjoy this latest edition. Feel free to forward any remaining questions concerning the publishing process to ron@publishingbasics.com.

    —Ron Pramschufer,
       February 2006

Is this the Introduction?

Yes, and beginning with the following paragraph, it is written by Ron Pramschufer, one of the founders of *SelfPublishing.com*. Please go ahead, Ron.

Thank you, Bob, I will.

While the printing process has changed dramatically over the past twenty years, the process of buying and selling printing has not changed much at all over the last hundred. The large conglomerate book printers print for the large conglomerate publishers. The second-tier book printers crave work from the same publishers that do business with the larger printers. They send their salesmen out to attract what they call "quality" publishers, ones that produce 50 to 100 titles per year.

So where does that leave the small press and independent self publishers? Too often they start out by taking their business to a smaller commercial printer that is not geared up for book production, but will at least make them feel like valued customers. The problem is that the cost is two or three times what is needed to compete effectively in the book marketplace.

Some self publishers are able to find an actual book manufacturer out of the 50,000 or so printers in the United States, but this generally doesn't work out much better. They wind up paying a significant premium because the marketing plans of these printers do not include small publishing companies or self publishers.

Why don't these book printers want to deal with self publishers? Here are some of the reasons printers have shared with me:

"They [self publishers] aren't sure what they want."
"They take up too much of the estimator's time."
"They don't understand the printing process."
"They don't bring us their work in the right format."
"Our salesmen spend too much time with them."
"Getting paid on a timely basis is often a problem."

What it boils down to is that you, the self publisher, represent an account that takes too much time and energy to service for the small amount of printing you buy. The printers want consistency and repeat business, and that's something that you, operating on your own, can't give them.

Enter *SelfPublishing.com*. Instead of your being one customer with one book, we combine you with hundreds of other customers and buy on your behalf as a single, unified customer. The key is standardization. Much like Goodyear Tire, *SelfPublishing.com* offers a limited number of sizes in a limited number of styles—tires off the rack, so to speak. One result of this standardization of product is that *SelfPublishing.com* buys at a significant discount and passes most of the savings on to you.

And our way of doing business solves all of the book printers' objections. First, because of our instant pricing function at the Web site, *SelfPublishing.com* jobs do not take up a minute of an estimator's time. *SelfPublishing.com* customers can still make all the specification changes they want, but they do it themselves at *SelfPublishing.com* the Web site. Second, *SelfPublishing.com* handles all the customer contact, so the printer deals with one experienced *SelfPublishing.com* person for dozens of books at any one time. Third, working with *SelfPublishing.com* ensures that all customer-furnished copy fits the printer's format. Any problems with files or artwork are sorted out and corrected long before they get to the printer. Fourth, there is no salesman and therefore no sales expense. *SelfPublishing.com* doesn't think you need to be sold anything. And finally, *SelfPublishing.com* customers pay in full for all their books by cash or credit card before they are shipped, so the printers, in turn, are happy to be paid promptly.

As an added bonus, *SelfPublishing.com* is not tied to any one technology. Our printer network includes digital printing houses, long- and short-run sheetfed printers, and web printers. These printers can efficiently handle anything from 100 copies to 100,000.

We treat all customers with respect, recognizing that you are the one hiring us to work for you. The same aggressive pricing applies to all customers equally.

We have designed this book to be an extremely useful resource for you. Please enjoy it, and good luck with all of your publishing projects. If you have additional questions, suggestions, or comments you'd like to share, please submit them directly to us at *SelfPublishing.com*.

—Ron Pramschufer

How difficult is it to publish my own book?

You can do it easily and do it well with the help provided here. You have probably produced a flyer or handout at some time in your life. If so, you already have some self publishing experience. Producing your completed book involves more work, of course, and you must overcome the inertia of just sitting there wishing you had a self published book.

To exorcise the demon of the self publishing doldrums, sing heartily to yourself. A song will spur and whip a lethargic mind to action. I'll even supply the words to your song:

> *Doubters and pessimists, come take a look!*
> *Yessirree, I'm going to publish my book.*
> *So dress me up and take me to the prom,*
> *Thanks for the help, SelfPublishing.com.*

Follow the advice on these pages and before long, your biggest problem just might be fending off the flunkies, flatterers, and parasites that dog the heels of the rich and famous.

What are some good reasons for self publishing?

First, you don't have to convince anybody but yourself that your book should be published. Making a good case to yourself for the publication of a work you have created should not be difficult at all. No one else shares the high degree of enthusiasm you have for your book. Why give a third party, with intentions, interests, and priorities different from your own, the final say? Self publishing gives you total control.

Second, if you have filled an existing void with your book and/or are able to create a demand for it, you will make more money than you would make with a standard publishing contract. Instead of a paltry 5% to 15% royalty, you'll make 20% to 80% of the purchase price. Once your self published book is successful, you can negotiate with a larger publisher from a position of experience and strength.

Third, you can see your book in print within a few weeks, or at most a few months, of your manuscript completion. The larger publishers most often work on an 18-month cycle, and that is just too long to wait.

Fourth, you can get distribution for your book through *Amazon.com* and *BarnesandNoble.com* just as easily as HarperCollins and Random House can for their books.

Fifth, you can preserve your own heritage—or that of your community, club, or whatever—in an inexpensive, quality format. Not everyone publishes to make a profit. Maybe you just want to leave a legacy with your family or share what you have learned with others.

Sixth, you can produce your book inexpensively through *SelfPublishing.com*.

What qualifies you to write a book like this?

I'm qualified because I did it. Here it is. You are reading it. In the same way, you will become qualified to write and publish your book by doing it.

I have much writing, editing, and publishing experience behind me, which helps. If you don't have that kind of experience, you learn from the experience of others, and read books like this to become qualified yourself. This book, in particular, leads you to (or back to) *SelfPublishing.com*, where you will find access to every resource you need to turn your desire to publish into a reality.

Why won't bookworms eat the pages of cartoon books?
They taste funny.

What is the story behind the development of this book?

I had self published two books and was working on several more when a friend told me about the *SelfPublishing.com* Web site. I saw on the home page that I could get an instant price on a book. I had a 176-page book in my computer formatted for the economical 5.5 x 8.5" trim size. I clicked my mouse a few times, filled in some blanks, and within two minutes I had a price. It had taken me, on the average, more than a week to get higher estimates on the same book from different printers around the country. *SelfPublishing.com* impressed me with its range, efficiency, and professionalism.

I searched the rest of the Web site and ordered their free book on the fundamentals of publishing. It was a good book, but it hadn't really caught up with the speed and convenience of *SelfPublishing.com*. I e-mailed Ron Pramschufer, one of the principals of the company, and suggested that I do a concise self publishing book for writers like you and me that would incorporate what *SelfPublishing.com* had to offer. Ron told me that he had been thinking about the same thing for a while, and we struck a deal. We agreed that we wanted to create a book that would complement the Web site and let you examine firsthand a number of different paper stocks and printing techniques offered through *SelfPublishing.com*. And here it is! Can't you now picture your own book beginning to make the transition from idea to reality?

What makes self publishing an attractive option?

The old saying "The first copy of your book costs a whole lot, but they're pretty inexpensive after that" is as true today as it was a hundred years ago. The setup charges are the same no matter what the quantity. The higher the setup cost, the larger the print run needed to amortize these costs into an acceptable unit cost.

Today's technology has reduced these setup costs whether you are printing a black-and-white novel or a full-color coffee table book. As little as fifteen years ago, typesetting made up a major portion of a book project's setup costs. Then, a standard 6 x 9" page cost between $6 and $10 to typeset and proofread. A project requiring two or three rounds of galley proofs and a set or two of page proofs could easily run that cost up to $15 or $20 per page. That meant that a 256-page book would cost $4,000 to $5,000 before you even got to the printer, which would then have to shoot and strip negatives at a cost of perhaps $7,500.

Today, the $600 computer with basic word processing software and the advent of PDF (Portable Document Format) has replaced the type houses of old. The laser printer has replaced expensive photo paper and chemicals. New computer-to-plate (CTP) techniques bypass film completely. The average savings to the small publisher amount to as much as $6,500 per title.

As a result, writers can put their own books into publication cost-effectively in relatively low quantities.

Should I start my own publishing company?

Absolutely. With the publishing of your first book, your activities in that regard become a publishing operation. You might as well name it and get a PO box. If you have a Mailboxes, Etc. location nearby, rent one of their boxes and your address will sound better: 1050 Pine Tree Boulevard, Suite 116, for example. Suite 116 at Mailboxes, Etc. is very, very small—but nobody will know that but you. You can even use your home address for your new publishing company. Just add "Suite 102" and the publishing giants will have nothing on you, address-wise.

You need a publishing company to get your ISBNs (International Standard Book Numbers) and LCCNs (Library of Congress Catalog Numbers) associated with you. You can get ten ISBNs for $225 plus a small handling charge. Be determined to use most of them if not all. Your first book may be good, but it just might be your fifth or sixth book that becomes a blockbuster! Once you have the experience of publishing your own book under your belt, you can help other writers get published—through your company, using one of your ISBNs.

Beware of companies that assist self publishers and claim to supply the ISBN and LCCN for your book for a small fee. These numbers will always be associated with them, not you!

Naming your company takes some thought. Don't be hokey, now! What do I mean by that? Naming my publishing company "Bob Johnson Publishing" would be hokey. Come up with a simple name that is easy to remember, is descriptive, and will not limit you in the future. If your first book is a children's book and you name your company "Child's

Play Publishing," for example, you won't be able to add teenage and adult books to your list without changing the name. Once you have narrowed your choices, check these resources in the library to avoid company name duplication: *Small Press Record of Books, Publishers Directory* by Gale Research, and *Books in Print*. Actually, the most important consideration in choosing a company name is whether or not the URL (*www.yourname.com*) is available. To check, go to *netsol.com*.

The basic business structures are sole proprietorship, partnership, and corporation. Most first-time publishers choose the sole proprietorship because it's the easiest to form.

Writing teacher: "Can you name two pronouns?"
Inattentive student: "Who, me?"

What is the difference between a vanity press, a subsidy press, and an on-demand publisher?

Linda and Jim Salisbury, the authors of *Smart Self Publishing,* define a subsidy press as "a publishing company that applies its ISBN to a book and charges the author for the cost of production. The author receives only a few copies of the book, and is promised royalties on those copies that might be sold by the subsidy press." They define a vanity press as "another term for a subsidy press. It implies that the published book has no value other than to stroke the author's ego." So a vanity press and a subsidy press are basically the same.

I responded to the ads for two subsidy presses in a national magazine and a week later received their introductory packets. Both of them were very slick and impressive—on the surface. I must commend the first one for its "Word of caution about financial returns." They write:

> No one can predict how a book will sell and, consequently, how much of your fee you are likely to regain by publishing your work with us. Some authors have received satisfactory returns. Others, however, did not find the market receptive and their financial rewards have been negligible. On the other hand, if financial success is not your prime concern, and if personal satisfaction ranks high in your desire for publication, then by all means consider [our subsidy publishing program].

If you have money to burn and only want a few books, this may be the way to go. If you don't have money to burn, the subsidy press process will work something like this: step 1, send in your manuscript for evaluation; step 2, sign a contract for between $10,000 and $15,000; step 3, go to the bank to get a second mortgage or use your 18% credit card to make the payment; step 4, get a few copies of your finished book; step 5, experience acute attacks of buyer's remorse while continuing to make payments on your mortgage or credit card for the next five or ten years. The second subsidy publisher was less up-front, but was pretty much the same story as the first.

On-demand publishers are another variation on the subsidy press/vanity press theme. On-demand publishers set up your digital manuscript to be printed one book at a time using a digital press. You pay a set fee of between $99 and $1,250 and receive in return one copy of your book. They set the retail price of the book, which is almost always higher than the normal market price, and allow you to buy books for yourself and friends at a discount. If they sell any books to retail outlets or through their Web sites, you receive a royalty. In reality, they sell very few books to anyone other than the author and their friends.

Here's an example. One company recently announced that it had paid its one-millionth dollar in royalty payments. If you figure an average book size of 256 pages and a royalty of $5.50 per book (their published rate), that comes to 181,000 books sold. That doesn't sound bad by itself. The trick comes when you dig a little further into their old press releases. They claim to have over 10,000 author/customers, and that same company proclaims over a million and a half books sold. You do the math. Eighteen copies sold to the "general public" compared to130 copies sold to the author. If that is what you have in mind, go for it. If not, read on.

What is a book coach, and how can one help me?

A book coach is a publishing consultant without the frills. A talented and dedicated book coach works closely with you to save you many hours of time, tons of frustration, and lots of money. As with everything else in the Internet publishing world, there are plenty of people out there waiting to pick your pocket. If you are going to hire a book coach, do your homework. Get references and in no case pay more than a couple hundred dollars for the service. *SelfPublishing.com* supplies a book coach to their customers who is available to answer general questions at no charge. His name is Bob Powers, and he can be reached at 800-479-1870 or Bob@rjcom.com.

What is e-publishing?

It's been a while since my initial research into e-book publishing. Since then most of the hype has died down, the venture capital money has dried up, most places are out of business, and the whole e-book "industry" has taken on the appearance of a corner three-card-monte game. The trade publications don't seem to be pumping out glowing accounts of the "e-book revolution" any more, probably because the advertising dollars have vanished, so why bother? During one of my visits to Book Expo America, I had the opportunity to talk to many of the remaining players in the e-book arena. The company I bought the original Stephen King e-novel from was still in business, but was not selling to the consumer any more; they were marketing their product only to libraries. The people from Amazon's Advantage program, who have always been good friends of the self publisher, told me that they were selling only technical e-books. After a little prodding as to why, I managed to get the most honest answer of the day concerning consumer e-books: "They just aren't selling." On the other hand, in a Publishing Basics Radio interview, the president of Lightning Source, a leading supplier of e-books, told me that e-book sales had grown to an amazing level. This book that you are reading is available in an e-book format. Many of you downloaded the e-book prior to ordering the printed copy.

The race is not over and it's hard to say exactly how it will turn out, but for now my advice is to save your money. It's less clear than ever whether the e-book will be the next CD or just another 8-track.

How do I get my work copyrighted?

The law grants you copyright protection automatically upon the creation of your work. Your work need not be completed to be protected. You own the copyright on your work as you create it. No publication or registration or other action in the U.S. Copyright Office is required to secure copyright. There are, however, definite advantages to registration. Among these are the following:

- Registration establishes a public record of the copyright claim.
- Before an infringement suit may be filed in court, registration is necessary for works of U.S. origin.
- If done before or within five years of publication, registration will establish prima facie evidence in court of the validity of the copyright and of the facts stated in the certificate.
- If registration is made within three months after publication of the work or prior to an infringement of the work, statutory damages and attorney's fees will be available to the copyright owner in court actions. Otherwise, only an award of actual damages and profits is available to the copyright owner.
- Registration allows the owner of the copyright to record the registration with the U.S. Customs Service for protection against the importation of infringing copies.

The copyright notice that appears in your published books should be similar to the one appearing on page 2 of this book. It should include the name of the copyright owner, the year of first publication, and the word "copyright" or the symbol ©.

When the copyright notice appears, an infringer cannot claim that he or she did not realize the work was protected.

You, as author and copyright owner, are wise to place a copyright notice on any unpublished copies of your work, or portions thereof that leave your control.

The use of the copyright notice is your responsibility and does not require advance permission from, or registration with, the Copyright Office.

Your copyright lasts from the moment of your work's creation (when it first appears in tangible form) until 70 years after your death. The copyright for a work prepared jointly by two or more authors lasts for 70 years after the last surviving author's death.

The copyright registration fee is $30 (as of November 2005). If you have any trouble with the registration process, you can use a service such as *ClickandCopyright.com* for a small fee to file your copyright for you.

How do I find the copyright symbol on my computer?

Every good word processor today gives you access to important characters that do not appear on the keyboard. They are called ANSI and ASCII character sets. To get the © character, make sure the Num Lock key on the right-hand side of your keyboard is on, and use those numbers for coding the character (the numbers at the top of the keyboard will not work). Now, hold down the Alt key and press 0169. When you release the Alt key, © will appear where your cursor is. From one writer to another, I am happy to present the access numbers to the following very useful set of characters hiding in your computer:

^	094	‰	0137	~	0126
•	0149	™	0153	œ	0156
¢	0162	©	0169	§	0167
£	0163	®	0174	µ	0181
¶	0182	±	0177	°	0176
1/4	0188	1/2	0189	3/4	0190
¿	0191	À	0192	Á	0193
Â	0194	Ã	0195	Ä	0196
Å	0197	Æ	0198	C	0199
È	0200	É	0201	Ê	0202
Ë	0203	Ì	0204	Í	0205
Î	0206	Ï	0207	x	0208
Ñ	0209	Ò	0210	Ó	0211
Ô	0212	Õ	0213	Ö	0214
Ø	0216	Ù	0217	Ú	0218
Û	0219	Ü	0220	x	0221

x	0222	ß	0223	à	0224
á	0225	â	0226	ã	0227
ä	0228	å	0229	æ	0230
ç	0231	è	0232	é	0233
ê	0234	ë	0235	ì	0236
í	0237	î	0238	ï	0239
x	0240	ñ	0241	ò	0242
ó	0243	ô	0244	õ	0245
ö	0246	÷	0247	ø	0248
ù	0249	ú	0250	û	0251
ü	0252	x	0253	x	0254

and my favorites: – (en dash) 0150 and — (em dash) 0151.

Since I've been using these symbols, I don't know how I ever got along without them. I'd feel especially lost without the em dash—I really would. And what a pleasure, instead of writing "resume," to be really cool and write "résumé."

On an older Mac, use key caps (under the apple) and press the Option key, the Command key, and the shift key to find the character you want. If you're running System 10, it's a little trickier. In Panther, launch System Preferences and choose the International preference. Click the Input Menu tab and enable the Input Menu option. When you do so, the Show Input Menu in Menu Bar option is enabled and the Input menu appears in the Finder. To reveal the Keyboard Viewer window, just select Keyboard Viewer from the Input menu. (That's if you're not using one of the excellent font utility programs available—Font Reserve™ or Suitcase™.)

What is an International Standard Book Number (ISBN)?

The International Standard Book Number (ISBN) is a number that uniquely identifies books and book-like products published internationally. The purpose of the ISBN is to establish and identify one title or edition of a title from one specific publisher. The ISBN is unique to that edition, allowing for more efficient marketing of products by booksellers, libraries, universities, wholesalers, and distributors.

If you have established your own publishing company—basically, a name and an address to begin with—you can purchase ISBNs from R.R. Bowker, the U.S. agency licensed to sell them. They cost $225 plus a small handling fee for a minimum of ten numbers. The usual turnaround time is ten business days for non-priority processing. For an additional fee, your application can be processed in three business days. If you are producing both paperback and hardback versions of your book, you will need two different ISBN numbers to identify them. To get all the details directly from R.R. Bowker, including the required forms, go to *SelfPublishing.com* and click "Obtaining an ISBN" on the home page.

The ISBN is printed on the copyright page of hardback and softback books, and on the lower portion of the back cover of a softback book above the bar code. Some major publishers place the ISBN on the back cover of their hardback books, and some don't.

For inclusion in *Books in Print*, be sure to put your ISBN on all your promotional literature.

Do I really need my own ISBN?

Yes. The ISBN is what identifies you as the publisher. Once you have obtained your ISBNs from R.R. Bowker, you are no longer a "self publisher." You are a "publisher" . . . an independent publisher. There is no difference at that point between you and Random House except for the fact that Random House publishes more titles than you (more than most publishers, for that matter). You assign one of these numbers to your first book. Once you own the ISBN, it remains the same for the life of the book. You can change printers, distributors, wholesalers, retailers, or whatever else you want—the book remains yours. If, ten years from now, someone orders a copy of your book, you, as the publisher, will get the order. If you don't own the number, the person who does will get the order.

"What's your first name, Mr. Hemingway?" the little boy asked earnestly.

Can't I have someone assign me one of their ISBNs?

No. The most common tactic used by today's vanity/subsidy presses is to tell you that they will "assign" or "sell" you an ISBN. They lead you to believe that your book is registered in your name and reinforce this by telling you "You retain all the rights." This is all double-talk. Nobody can give or assign you a number. They can let you use one of their numbers, but you do not own it. The orders for that book (ISBN) will always go to that publisher. If you change publishers (and I use that term loosely), the ISBN does not go with you; it remains theirs. You will need to start all over with your marketing efforts under your new ISBN number. Even worse than the vanity presses are a new group of companies that present themselves as resellers of single ISBNs. One in particular sells bar codes as a regular business and is even recommended on various sites for being a bar code supplier. I talked with the owner of this company about his selling of single numbers. He out-and-out lied to me, and I even introduced myself as being in the business. When I called R.R. Bowker, they told me that they were starting legal proceedings against this company, but in the meantime unsuspecting authors are being taken in every day. Remember: *There is no company in the United States that can sell you a legitimate ISBN identifying you as the publisher except for R.R. Bowker*. Anyone who tells you different is pulling your leg.

What about bar codes?

The ISBN for your book is easily translated into a globally compatible bar code format called a Bookland EAN (European Article Number). Every bookstore chain and most smaller bookshops use bar code scanning at the checkout register. If you didn't know that, you haven't been to a bookstore in the last ten years, and I'd say it's time for you to visit one.

Putting the bar code on your book is part of the book cover designer's job, and it's a simple one. Using a software program, the designer types in your ISBN, and the bar code comes up in just the right place on your back cover. You can put your book's retail price near the bar code on the back cover if you want to. That doesn't mean that retailers will always have to charge the full amount. Using their computers, they can tie your Bookland EAN code to a sale price, and that's what will appear on the register when your book is scanned.

If you are using a bar code, it must be black or a color dark enough to be scanned. Keep this in mind when counting the number of colors on your cover. It is not necessary to buy bar codes from R.R. Bowker when you buy your ISBNs. Your cover designer should have the software needed to generate a bar code. No matter where you buy the bar code, don't pay more than $25 for it.

At the bookstore, I asked the salesperson, "Where's the self-help section?"
She said, "If I told you it would defeat the purpose."

Image section:
Printed web offset on 50# white offset, 512ppi.

For details on the printing process, see pages 84-87. Actual paper shade may vary from printer to printer. The same images on these pages appear in other sections of the book for comparison.

Helvetica thin	12 on 18 leading	15% black background
Helvetica thin	12 on 18 leading	no background
Helvetica	12 on 18 leading	30% black background
Helvetica	12 on 18 leading	no background
Helvetica medium	12 on 18 leading	60% black background
Helvetica medium	12 on 18 leading	no background
Helvetica black	12 on 18 leading	75% black background
Helvetica black	12 on 18 leading	no background
Helvetica black	12 on 18 leading	100% black background

Chapter 23

Chapter 24

EDITORIAL QUESTIONS

Where can I get writing help?

All you have to do is search the *SelfPublishing.com* Web site for connections. There you will find all kinds of writing clubs and societies eager to help members improve their skills. I especially recommend these ten books:

- *On Writing Well,* by William Zinsser. An informal guide to writing nonfiction.
- *If You Want to Write,* by Brenda Ueland. A book about art, independence, and spirit.
- *The Writer's Chapbook,* edited from *Paris Review* interviews and with an introduction by George Plimpton. A compendium of fact, opinion, wit, and advice from the twentieth century's preeminent writers.
- *The Elements of Editing,* by Arthur Plotnik. A modern guide for editors and journalists. Editing is writing.
- *Woe Is I,* by Patricia T. O'Conner. The grammarphobe's guide to better English in plain English.
- *12 Keys to Writing Books That Sell,* by Kathleen Krull. A mirror that will help you see the strengths and weaknesses in your writing.
- *Technique in Fiction,* by Robie Macauley and George Lanning. An imaginative rather than mechanical approach to a complicated subject, featuring a splendid variety of examples.

- *The Writer's Digest Handbook of Novel Writing,* from the editors of *Writer's Digest.* Practical advice and instruction for creating a novel.
- *100,000 Plus Power Phrases for Students, Writers, Speakers, and Business People,* by Robert Bowie Johnson, Jr. A study of ideas and a stimulant to deep and original thinking.

You can find these and other excellent books on writing at, or through, the *SelfPublishing.com* online bookstore.

Whether you think you need writing help or not, I highly recommend that you subscribe to *Writer's Digest* magazine. They call their classifieds the "Writer's Mart," and it's worth the price of the subscription just to have access to that. There you can find writing classes, conferences, and contests; editing, critiquing, and ghostwriting services; and much more. When you get your *Writer's Digest* each month in the mail, you'll remember that you subscribe to it because you are a writer! It's easy to forget that sometimes, believe me.

You can reach the *Writer's Digest* Web site under Trade Publications in the "Step 1: Education" section of *SelfPublishing.com.* There are also many different Internet-based writers groups, most of which offer free newsletters. My personal favorites are *absolutewrite.com* and *SPAWN.org.*

Good: Your diligent editing uncovers 99 errors in your writing. Bad: After it's published.

Where should I go for critiquing help?

If you want to save money, try to get a qualified friend to help you. Perhaps you can find an English teacher or graduate student at a nearby college who would be willing to help in exchange for acknowledgment in your book. Members of local writers groups often help each other with editing.

SelfPublishing.com has an excellent Editorial Analysis program. For under $200, a publishing professional reviews your manuscript for the following:

- The appropriateness of the content for the intended readership
- Grammar
- Punctuation
- Syntax
- Style and content of notes, bibliographies, references, and citations
- Permissions
- Art and figures

The author receives a report from the editor along with a sample edit as well as a recommendation as to how much editing is needed to bring your manuscript up to commercial standards. If you agree with the editor and proceed with the recommended editing, your entire analysis fee is applied as a rebate against the upcoming editing charge. Even if you choose not to follow the advice of the analysis, it is still a worthwhile investment.

What about copy editing and proofreading?

Finding errors after a work is published torments the soul of a writer in much the same way as malevolent phantoms agonize a paranoid imagination. It's a problem you can avoid by making the time, and spending the money if necessary, to be sure your work is correct.

Copy editors check written material to correct errors in grammar, spelling, usage, and style, usually as the next-to-last step before the work is sent to the designer. At *SelfPublishing.com* we break editorial services into four basic levels. Levels 1 and 2 are basically the same, except that a Level 2 copy edit involves more corrections than a Level 1. In **Levels 1 and 2** our editor will:

- Correct errors in grammar and punctuation.
- Correct average to minor errors in syntax (i.e., the ordering of and relationship between the words and other structural elements in a phrase or sentence).
- Query phrasing and word choices deemed inappropriate for the subject matter or readership.
- Flag instances where permission from an outside source may be needed.
- Correct common errors involving familiar subjects, such as changing *The Johnny Carson Show* to *The Tonight Show Starring Johnny Carson.*

Our editor will not:
- Restructure beyond minor sentence and phrase structure adjustments.
- Significantly alter word choices. We will, however,

suggest that the author change these items to make them more appropriate to the readership.

Levels 3 and 4 are more substantive edits compared with the "mechanical" edit of Levels 1 and 2. For all levels, you will receive your manuscript back with all comments from the editor, and you may accept or reject the changes. If you feel that you need a dialogue with the editor or that the editor should look at your manuscript again, Level 4 is what you need. In **Level 3** our editor will:

- Correct errors in grammar and punctuation.
- Correct errors in syntax with regard to sentence structure. In certain instances, the editor may suggest that the author change the sentence structure in order to preserve the intended meaning.
- Alter phrases and word choices deemed inappropriate for the subject matter or readership.
- Flag instances where permission from an outside source may be needed.
- Promote accuracy of content by providing light research as warranted. (e.g., look up biblical quotes, common statistics, etc.).
- Preserve plot line, character traits, and consistency.
- Flag minor instances where the material strays from the intended purpose.
- Prepare development documents to maintain plot line and character traits in fiction titles.
- For nonfiction manuscripts, the editor will preserve consistency throughout by noting the author's individual theories, title-specific terminology, and so on.

Our editor will not:

- Reorganize paragraphs to make the structure more logical to the reader. If this is required, a heavy substantive edit is more appropriate.
- Provide a full fact check for the document. Only easily verified facts are checked by the editor.

With a **Level 4** copy edit, you will receive your manuscript back with all comments from the editor, and you may accept or reject the changes. You then submit your manuscript again to the editor and it is looked at a second time, allowing you, in effect, to have a dialogue with the editor.

For a nonfiction submission our editor will:

- Provide a full editorial read-through of the material.
- Correct mechanical errors in spelling, grammar, and syntax.
- Analyze the targeted readership, purpose, and uses of the work to determine if the content is complete and appropriate. The editor will help you to eliminate erroneous or irrelevant information.
- Ensure that concepts are developed adequately and that the material is well organized.
- Check all figures for appropriateness. If any figures are considered inappropriate, our editor will query.
- Provide light fact checking of material in question.
- Flag instances where permission from an outside source may be needed.

- Offer additional suggestions for improving the work and recommend revisions where appropriate
- Maintain a full style sheet to preserve consistency throughout by noting the author's individual theories, title-specific terminology, and so on.
- Make changes necessary to produce a publishable title by industry standards.
- Provide a summary of main developmental issues in the manuscript.
- Review the manuscript following client review to ensure that all queries have been addressed and to accept all tracked changes.

Our editor will not:

- Make significant changes that alter the meaning of the text or change the direction of the plot.
- Provide a full fact check of the material. If this is requested or required, a separate fact-checking service is available.

For fiction submissions our editor will:

- Provide a full editorial read-through of the material.
- Correct mechanical errors in spelling, grammar, and syntax.
- Analyze the targeted readership to determine if the content is complete and appropriate, and. help to remove erroneous or irrelevant information.
- Provide light fact checking of material in question.
- Flag instances where permission from an outside

source may be needed.

- Flag instances where the material strays from the plot line.
- Offer suggestions intended to improve the work.
- Maintain a full style sheet to preserve consistency throughout by tracking character development and important plot points.
- Check all figures for appropriateness.
- Provide a summary of main developmental issues in the manuscript.

Our editor will not:

- Make significant changes that will alter the meaning of the text or change the direction of the plot.
- Provide a full fact check of the material. If this is desired, please inquire for an estimate.

Pricing for any level of editing is done on a per-word basis so that you know exactly what your charges are going to be. You should avoid editors who want to charge you by the hour or page. If you agree to pay by the hour, you might have a fast editor or a slow editor and you will receive a mystery invoice at the end. As for per-page charges, the definition of a page is a little different depending on the editor. Payment per word is easy. All you need to do to determine how many words you have is go to the Tools menu in MS Word and choose Word Count from the drop-down. It's easy.

What word processing program should I use?

Stick with the big two: Microsoft Word or WordPerfect. Both of these programs check your spelling and grammar and offer an excellent thesaurus. These are now the standard word processors in the e-world. Using a different software program for word processing is like typing a manuscript on colored paper: There is no advantage or point to it.

Try to avoid an abbreviated version of the real thing that comes loaded for free with many computers. There is a reason why it's free.

Remember: Book manufacturers do not print from word processing files. All files must be converted to an acceptable format.

Writer: "I'm not up to writing today, sweetheart. I fell through the front door screen."
Spouse: "Oh, you poor dear! You've strained yourself."

Sample book covers from SelfPublishing.com's design service.

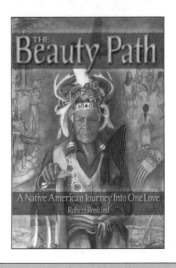

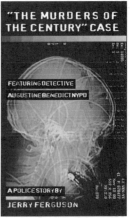

DESIGN QUESTIONS

What typeface should I use for my text?

If you are doing your own layout, you should use a serif typeface, or font, if you want your text to be easy to read. Serifs are the small extensions or "ticks" on the bases and tops of letters. They lead the eye from one letter to the next, making the type easier to read. The typeface for this book is Veljovik Book, an elegant serif font. Many authors use Times New Roman because it is the default font in Microsoft Word. For book printing Times New Roman is somewhat unpredictable, however, and you won't find many books in a store that use this font. Better to avoid it if you can.

If you want something different, I suggest Century Schoolbook, Baskerville, Garamond, Goudy Old Style, or another easily readable serif font. Avoid sans serif fonts— "sans" from the French, meaning "without." This sentence is written in Arial, a sans serif typeface, and reading several pages of it will tire your eyes. Serif fonts are good for body copy, and sans serif fonts are good for headers and subheaders, which is the scheme we've used throughout this book.

The designers at *SelfPublishing.com* will assist you with type selection and overall layout of your book if you think you need help.

What margins do you recommend?

Probably the thing that amateurs neglect most often is to allow enough space for margins. The printer requires white space all around the page, including around running heads and folios. We suggest a minimum of 0.5" of white space in the gutter (center of the book) and 0.375" on the other three sides. You should never have anything in print closer than 0.25" to the edge of your trim.

How do I prepare my text for the printer?

One of the most significant changes that has taken place since the first printing of this book is the file format most requested by book printers. Adobe PDF appears to have won the race when it comes to preferred text format. It works with virtually all imagesetters, platesetters, and digital output devices. Most popular file formats, including MS Word, WordPerfect, and MS Publisher, can be converted to PDF. Like PostScript, PDF is a "locked" format, so there usually is no problem with reflows when the files are opened on different computers. A PDF document can be read by Acrobat Reader or an equivalent. Acrobat Reader is available for free at the Adobe Web site and *SelfPublishing.com*, and many Internet sites have links for downloadable readers. Adobe has made PDF creation even easier by offering a file conversion service at *adobe.com* for $9.95 per month (which can be canceled at any time).

Like everything else in the electronic world, the meaning of the word "easy" is relative. It may take a little time and patience, but for all you Word users, it's certainly easier and cheaper than purchasing and learning to use PageMaker or QuarkXpress. Of course, if you'd like, you can do what I did and hire Jonathan Gullery at *SelfPublishing.com*, who, for a reasonable fee, will lay out your book in the proper format. Since our computers save us thousands of dollars in typesetting costs, we should be able to afford several hundred dollars for the services of someone who specializes in ensuring that our books make it from PC to press smoothly and efficiently.

At the *SelfPublishing.com* Web site there are tips on how to convert a file yourself—if you choose to go that route.

When is a good time to use Microsoft Word to lay out my book?

Simply put . . . Never! Microsoft anything does not work very well with any printing process except your desktop printer. Bill Gates started out as a computer geek, not a commercial book printer. Word and WordPerfect are both word processing programs. As such they both do a good job of processing words. Spell checker, grammar checker, thesaurus—all great tools to help you write a better manuscript. However, when it's time to turn your manuscript into a book, you will be wasting a lot of time and effort by trying to make a word processing program act like a page layout program.

The primary problem is that the way Word behaves on your machine depends on your printer drivers. What looks great on your screen may look entirely different on another computer with a whole different set of printer drivers. Your carefully positioned headers can suddenly move to the next page! A Word document can be converted to a PDF document (a file format that commercial printers can use), but you usually encounter the same problem in making the conversion. A 256-page Word document can suddenly turn into a 292-page PDF document. You may struggle for dozens of hours trying to jerry-rig your document to "look" like the book layout on your screen, only to find that once you convert the file to PDF for printing, the result is a jumbled mess.

If you really have the urge to design and lay out your book, you'll need to invest in a page layout program like Quark or PageMaker and learn how to use it. These are fairly expensive programs and not particularly easy for the novice to understand. I do know plenty of authors, though, who have gone this way and found the experience to be personally rewarding. If this doesn't sound exciting, however, you can do a little shopping and discover that the price to have your book professionally designed and laid out does not cost as much as buying a layout program. In my opinion, you will be much better off saving yourself the money, time, and aggravation and investing it in a marketing program for your book.

My personal favorite designer is Jonathan Gullery, whom I have been working with for over twenty years. He is quite talented, easy to work with, and charges a very reasonable price. You can get a complete design and layout of a 256-page book for under $500. He will design a book cover or dust jacket for about the same price. You can visit him at *SelfPublishing.com*.

All that said, a do-it-yourself section was recently added to the *SelfPublishing.com* Web site. There are some templates there as well as some articles by Jack Lyon on how to lay out your book in MS Word. This section was added in response to the hundreds of calls received from individuals who would prefer to spend countless hours trying to do their own layout as opposed to having a book laid out by a professional for a couple hundred dollars. Preferably, you should spend your time figuring out how you are going to market your books, but if you insist, the section is there for anyone printing a few hundred copies.

It's that 99% of the vanity presses that give the rest a bad name!

Can I supply camera copy?

Ten years ago I would have answered, "Of course! It costs about $10 per page for camera work, film, and layout." Five years ago I would have answered, "Sure, but it will cost you $5 per page to scan your laser proofs into a digital format." Today the answer is just "Sure!" Most printers today have scanners that will scan in excess of 30 pages per minute. A 320-page book takes about 10 minutes to scan. In short . . . it's no big deal. Some printers still have slower scanners and need to charge a couple dollars per page, but the marketplace is going to force these printers into line with the ones that are not charging at all. Remember, though, scanning your laser copy puts the final printing another generation away from the original in a quality manner. But for straight text with no halftones (pictures) or screened graphics, few people will know the difference. I suggest that if you are leaning in that direction, you go out and buy a ream of good paper (you know the kind I mean) and set your printer to as high a dpi as possible and give it a whirl. For books with screens or halftones you still need to figure out how to get your files converted to a PDF format. You'll be happy you did.

What kind of proofs will I see?

Let me answer that by first going back thirty-five years or so in the printing industry. Then, writers used manual typewriters to create their manuscripts and Linotype operators set type in hot metal. There were several different proof stages before a book got to the printer. The first stage was the galleys. Individual lines of type were keyed in and molded in metal on a Linotype machine. A line of type was as thick as the point size, as long as the specified column width, and about half an inch high. That was the "line of type." Compositors placed these lines of type in long trays called galleys, line by line, and locked them together to keep them from falling apart. The term "leading" came from the slivers of lead put between the lines of type to space them out on the page. With an order to "increase the leading" a compositor physically added strips of lead in between the lines.

Once all the type was in place in the galleys, an ink impression of them was taken on long paper sheets, and these were called the galley proofs. They were then proofread, and corrections made. If a line of type contained an error, the old slug of type for that line was removed and a new line was created and inserted. Corrections at this stage were fairly inexpensive; it was not uncommon to go through two or three sets of galley proofs before going to the next step.

Once the writer or editor approved the final galley proofs, a designer pasted them into page layouts. Based on those layouts, the compositor took the galleys of metal type and composed them into page trays, leaving spaces for the placement of halftones (pictures), maps, charts, pen-and-ink drawings, and so on, which were dropped in later by the printer. Once these pages were locked, the page proofs were printed from the composed pages of type. Changes at this stage of the process were much more expensive.

After the page proof was approved, a camera-ready reproduction proof, or repro proof, was made from the same metal page type. Repro proofs were printed on better paper, and special attention was given to print quality because the approved repro proofs were sent to the printer to make negatives for offset printing.

Once the printer received the camera-ready repro proof, he photographed it on a litho camera and made film negatives. These negatives were then taped, or stripped, onto large imposition sheets called film flats. Their layout corresponded to the position of the pages on the press sheet. (A 6 x 9" book with sixty-four pages was typically printed as two 32-page sections, or signatures, on a 38 x 50" sheet of paper.) At this stage, the printer made another proof by exposing the film flats on photographic paper that was developed in a chemical solution, and then hung on a clothesline to dry. When the photosensitive paper developed, the type appeared as dark blue on a white background. Thus the term "blueline" came into existence. The proof paper could only be developed on one side, so the pages were glued together, back to back, to show the actual layout of the book. A folded and trimmed book of glued-together bluelines functioned as the final proof before going to press. Printers referred to this book of bluelines as the bookblue.

Making corrections at the bookblue stage of production was quite expensive. If an editor caught a minor typographical error, the typesetter had to set a new line of type to replace the flawed one in the page tray. He then had to make another repro proof before the printer shot another negative and stripped that correction into the film flats.

Why am I telling you all this when the only Linotype machines remaining are either in museums or perhaps somewhere in the New York Times or Chicago Tribune building waiting for the last union Linotype operator to retire? The reason I've gone into such detail is that we cling to many of the terms from that bygone era, and, out of habit, we sometimes expect to see certain proofs that not only are unnecessary, but no longer exist!

Today, you, as the writer, create the equivalent of galleys as you type away at your word processor. Back in the old days, you didn't dare change the column width because it meant resetting the entire manuscript. Today, you can change the column width in a few seconds, and make any other changes you want right there on the screen in front of you. Hit your print button and you've got a galley proof that you can read on the train, or in bed, or carry around in your briefcase to show your friends. Format your type into actual pages and print them, and you've got your page proofs. You can even use your laser printer to print them front and back, just as they will appear in your book.

You're in charge now. You and your computer have replaced the old prepress process.

What kind of text proof will I receive?

The final proofs that printers offer today vary depending on the printing method. *SelfPublishing.com* makes sure each customer gets a final proof that is compatible with the printing technology used for his or her book. These final printer proofs are your last chance to catch mistakes before you go to press. Funny things can happen between your initial type input and the time when your book reaches the printing press. The obvious thing to check at this stage is that all the pages are there and are all in the right order. Some of the not-so-obvious things to check are to make sure that no formatting changes occurred when you converted to PDF from your application program. Punctuation sometimes changes, and fonts also sometimes change. It's up to you to catch these problems in the proof. Once you have OK'd the proof, you have bought the books that match that proof. We had a case in one of the printings of this book where we gave the identical PDF file to five printers to print the five signatures on five different presses. When printed, four of the five were perfect. The fifth was missing all the punctuation marks. In the end, we had to pay for the incorrect pages because we had seen the proof. The fact that four other printers took the exact same file and printed it perfectly meant nothing. Don't let this happen to you. Check your proof.

As a successful self publisher, always try to be modest.
And be damn proud of it!

What kind of cover proof will I receive?

Your designer's computer is capable of doing things that only a decade ago were reserved for prepress film houses with millions of dollars worth of equipment. Today, in most cases, when your designer finishes your cover, it's ready for press.

If you are running a one- or two-color cover, your designer's laser proof should be enough. The printer will print the PMS (Pantone Matching System) colors that you specify on your order.

With a four-color cover, things are a little different. You should not rely on your designer's laser proof unless you have a fairly wide window of tolerance between your proof and the printed cover. You should also never count on what you see on your computer screen to be more than a general representation of what will be printed on the final product. But what can you rely on?

Your best color proof is a press proof, but domestic printers rarely supply these because of their prohibitive cost. The next best proof is a film proof like a chromalin or matchprint. This type of proof consists of four layers of color film exposed from the negatives used to make the printing plates, mounted on top of each other on paper, giving the full color appearance. The problem here is that the trend in printing is moving away from negatives toward direct-to-plate. No negative, no film proof. That leaves us with a digital proof. Over the past several years, digital proofs have gained widespread acceptance. They are not as good as press proofs or film proofs, but that's progress. Remember that no one but you has seen your original cover. The money you save using today's technology far outweighs any minor color variation in the final product.

Should I have my book cover professionally designed?

Yes. It is worth every penny. The next time you're in the bookstore, take the time to examine the cover designs. I can write with confidence that ninety-nine out of every one hundred of those book covers were professionally designed. If there are exceptions to this rule, they will be found in the bookstore section featuring local authors, and nine out of ten of those books will have covers designed by people who knew what they were doing.

Normally, you are attracted to a person because of his or her face. The cover is your book's face. Acne, bed-head, and snarled lips discourage interest in your book, if you get the analogy.

What is the difference between a cover, a jacket, and a casewrap?

These are related in that they all print and wrap around the text pages of your book. A cover is the term we use to describe what wraps around a paperback book. Jackets and casewraps are on hardcover books. The difference here is that a jacket is loose (i.e., it can be removed from the book) and has flaps. Casewraps are more like a cover in that they wrap the binder boards, which are what wraps your text pages. Casewraps are typically used on children's books, field guides, school textbooks, cookbooks and short-run hardcover guides.

Do I need to use four colors to create an effective cover/jacket/casewrap?

There is no black or white answer to this question! Look at your own books. Some of them, I'm sure, have very attractive two-color covers. The designer who did them really had three colors to work with since the white of the paper was already there, so they actually had a whole variety of color shades to work with. It's possible to save some money using a well-designed one- or two-color cover.

You might think that the printing cost difference between one-, two-, and four-color covers would be substantial, but the industry has changed, and four-color covers are most often only a few cents more than one- or two–color covers. While two-color covers can be nice, spend some time in a bookstore looking at different covers. If there are two travel books, one with a two-color and the other with a four-color cover, which one do you think looks more attractive? Keep in mind that there is no two-color option in digital printing; it's either black or four-color, similar to your desktop printer at home.

Remember that if you are using a bar code, it must be black or a color dark enough to be scanned. Keep this in mind when counting the number of colors on your cover. Building your bar code out of different colors is not a very good idea—you'll find very few books with anything other than black bar codes.

How do I know how wide the spine will be?

There's a simple formula that determines the spine width. Just take the number of pages in your book and divide that figure by your text paper's ppi (pages per inch). Where do you get the ppi? It depends on what kind of paper you're using, and it usually appears on the printer's estimate or quote. If for some reason it doesn't appear there, ask the printer for it, or see the spine width calculator in the Production Center at *SelfPublishing.com*.

Let's say your book has 200 pages and you are printing it on a web press using novel news, which has a ppi of 400. Then the width of your book's spine will be 200 ÷ 400, or half an inch. That's for a paperback. For a hardcover book, you have to allow for the thickness of the boards. The easiest way to do this accurately is to have your printer provide you with a template. Templates are available at *SelfPublishing.com* in the Production Center.

Secretary: "Sir, there's an invisible writer at the door."
Editor: "Tell him I can't see him now."

How do I prepare my cover/jacket/casewrap for the printer?

Let's deal with the front, the spine, and the back of the cover in that order. On the front, put the book title, the subtitle, and the author. Place any graphics you want here. On the spine, the author's last name is usually at the top, the book title is in the center, and the publisher is identified at the bottom. On the back put a four-sentence description of your book. You can put endorsements here, too. Leave space for a very short bio on the author, a photograph of the author, and the ISBN and bar code.

These are the traditional places to put all of these things, but, of course, you can break any or all of the rules whenever you want! Remember, however, that you do want to sell your book, so people have to know very quickly why they should buy it.

If you are designing your cover, make sure you have some "bleed." If your artwork goes all the way to the edge, it must extend at least one-eighth inch more, so that when the book is trimmed there will be no white showing. This extra one-eighth inch is the "bleed." Our designers usually provide about a quarter inch bleed to be safer. Remember that if you are using a bar code, it must be black or a color dark enough to be scanned. Avoid making small type a color. Cut out the cover and wrap it around a book on your shelf. How does it look now?

When you put your cover on disc, you must include all the fonts and graphics you have used. It's also a good idea to include any items that have been embedded in other programs during the design process. Then, if there's something wrong, it will be easier to fix.

If you are having a designer create the cover, explain clearly what you would like to see. You can also just give a designer an idea of what's in your book and let the expert go for it! If you have covers you really like, copy them and send them along. Remember, though, you are hiring a designer, not commissioning an artist to create an original work for you. A designer at *SelfPublishing.com* told me a story about one customer who wanted a cover showing a cave halfway up a mountain, a bear and a donkey sitting on a nearby ledge, symbols from the I Ching surrounding the door of the cave, and the moon setting behind the mountain! What the author needed in this case, they concluded, was not a cover designer but an illustrator. In cases like this, the illustrator and designer work together to achieve the final desired result.

A good designer will take your concept and give you something that will work. Remember, despite what you have heard, you *can* sometimes judge a book by its cover.

Editor: "I'll hire you at $300 a week and up it to $600 a week in six months."
Writer: "I think I'll just come back in six months."

For details on the printing process, see pages 84-87. Actual paper shade may vary from printer to printer. The same images on these pages appear in other sections of the book for comparison.

Helvetica thin	12 on 18 leading	15% black background
Helvetica thin	12 on 18 leading	no background
Helvetica	12 on 18 leading	30% black background
Helvetica	12 on 18 leading	no background
Helvetica medium	12 on 18 leading	60% black background
Helvetica medium	12 on 18 leading	no background
Helvetica black	12 on 18 leading	75% black background
Helvetica black	12 on 18 leading	no background
Helvetica black	12 on 18 leading	100% black background

Chapter 23

Chapter 24

MANUFACTURING QUESTIONS

What is a page?

Turn to page 1 in this book or any other book. Then turn the page. The back of page 1 is page 2. Then comes page 3, and the back of page 3 is page 4, and so on. Odd-numbered pages are always on the right, and even-numbered pages are always on the left. I know this seems obvious, but counting pages is one of the most misunderstood simple concepts in printing. Don't be fooled by thinking about "pages" and "leaves." If I tell you to turn to page 32, you just turn to page 32. You don't think, "Let's see . . . that's really the second side of leaf 16 . . ."; you just turn to page 32. This book has 136 pages, not 68.

SelfPublishing.com has received its share of manuscripts with the pages numbered 1F and 1B (1Front and 1Back), 2F and 2B, and so on—instead of 1, 2, 3, 4, . . . And yet has any of us ever seen a book in print with pages numbered 1F, 1B, 2F, 2B, 3F, 3B? Could it be mind-numbing x-rays emanating from the copy machines at Kinko's that are causing this confusion?

Remember that every page counts as a page whether it is blank or part of the text—numbered or not.

Is there a difference in appearance between a digitally produced book and one produced by standard offset printing?

Every time I listen to the Reader's Radio interview with Dan Poynter on "The New Book Model," I have to chuckle. Dan, of course, is the head guru of the small press publishing world. There aren't many small publishers who have not heard of his name or been to one of his seminars. While I agree with most of the things he says about publishing and marketing, I take exception with his opinion on the difference between digital and traditional offset printing. Dan states with authority, referring to digitally produced books, "They look just like any other book. . . . I challenge you to even tell the difference."

If you believe that the full-color printing in *USA Today* is equal to the color printing in *GQ* magazine (as many consumers do), you will probably not notice the difference between a book produced in a digital plant and one that was printed at an offset book manufacturer. Don't get me wrong. I am not saying that digital printing is bad. I am saying that it is different.

The modern digital color cover presses are very good. I threw away my "loupe" (magnifying glass used for checking registration and dot structure) years ago. Taking this into consideration, and the fact that my eyes aren't what they were thirty-five years ago when I got into the business, you can hardly tell the difference between a process color cover printed on a digital press and one printed on an offset press, as long as there is a film lamination on top of the printing. Without the lamination, it is pretty easy to tell the difference, but no experienced publisher would sell a book without a laminated cover. The main area that still needs improvement in the color digital process is that of solids or gradated screens. It is still fairly easy to see banding and other inconsistencies in these areas. Still, if I were to grade the overall cover appearance, I would give it a B+ versus an A for the offset cover (still on the honor roll).

Digital text printing has also come a long way. There are a couple of different processes in use, but the most common is DocuTech™ by Xerox®. In short, a Xerox® by any other name is still a Xerox®. For straight type, it looks fine. It's a much darker/denser black than offset because it's toner and not ink. It is almost an unnatural look after so many years of seeing ink on paper, although it certainly passes the "no loupe, no glasses" test.

The problem comes into play when you try to mix even the simplest graphics or halftones (images) into the text. There is no comparison between the appearance of graphics and halftones done on a digital press and those printed on a traditional offset press. Compare the same images and graphics on the different paper stocks, using both the digital presses and offset presses used in this book. You can see the difference yourself between the two processes.

Now that we have talked about some of the more obvious differences between digital and offset, we'll move on to some of the more subtle differences. Have you ever unpacked a ream of copy paper, loaded it into a copier, and run off 500 copies? Does the pile of "copies" have the same physical appearance as the pile of paper you loaded in the feeder tray? Ever try to put the 500 "copies" back into the same package that the 500 blank sheets of paper came from? Most digital processes utilize extreme temperatures to fuse the toner to the paper. This heat takes the moisture out of the paper, which tends to make the "copies" fresh out of the copier brittle. Natural humidity puts moisture back into the paper but not necessarily to the same degree as when it came out of the pack. If you leave the pile of "copies" out for a while, the pile will start to flatten but it will never get back to the condition it started at; thus the appearance of the paper will be slightly changed. The offset presses that print single-color books do not use heat. The sheet that goes into the press is the same sheet that comes out of the press. If you have seen a digital printing line in operation, you'll recall that the "book block" comes out of the copier and goes right into the binder. Now try to picture this pile of sheets (book block), with all the moisture drawn out of the sheets, being sealed on the binding edge with adhesive to apply the cover. You now have a book block picking up moisture on three sides and not the fourth. You can get a curl to the whole book that will never flatten out. This problem itself gives the overall finished book a C or C+ look, bringing the whole product down to a C+, which is still "commercially acceptable" but bothersome to many customers.

Another typical problem lies in the strength of the binding. In perfect binding, signatures (groups of pages) are gathered to make a book block. The binding edge goes through a grinding unit, which "roughs up" the edge so the adhesive will hold better when the cover is applied to the binding edge of the book. After the cover is applied and wrapped around the book, the book block gets trimmed on the outside, top, and bottom by either a three-knife trimmer or a flatbed cutter, making a finished book. A typical new perfect binding machine used by offset book manufacturers can cost over two million dollars. The perfect binders that are used in digital shops cost as little as $20,000 and rarely more than $100,000. The difference between the two types involves a lot more than markup. Most binders used by digital printers produce little more than a glorified pad. Ninety-five percent of the complaints that I have run into with the digital product revolve around the binding, and 75% of them concern the pages falling out as the book is flattened out for reading.

As long as I am on the topic of pages falling out, I might as well talk about the main cause of this problem. Aside from the problems of inefficient grinding units and the cheaper binders applying adhesives, the main culprit is the grain of the paper. Paper is made primarily of pulp and water (as well as chemicals to regulate brightness and opacity). As the paper-making process begins, pulp is added to water to make a sort of pulp soup. As this solution moves through the papermaking machine, the pulp fibers line up in parallel rows. Moisture is removed until the mixture becomes paper. (Any paper people reading this, please excuse my simplistic description of this process.) The bottom line is that the direction in which these pulp fibers are aligned represents the "grain" of the paper. All paper has a grain. If you take a piece of 8.5 x 11" copy paper and fold it the 11" way, you get a nice, smooth fold. Fold the same sheet the 8.5" way and you get a ragged, irregular fold. The heavier the paper, the more pronounced this effect. You always want the grain of the paper to run parallel to the binding edge of the book. This allows the pages of the book to open naturally. If the grain is going against the bind, the book does not lay open naturally. The reader will tend to "flatten" the book to keep it from "snapping" shut. As the book is repeatedly flattened, the spine eventually breaks. Once this happens, the pages start falling out of the book.

Most digital presses print an 8.5 x 11" sheet of paper. Except for special orders, the grain of the paper is 11". That yields a wrong-grain 5.5 x 8.5" book. If short-grain paper is specially ordered so that the 5.5 x 8.5" product is correct, it yields a wrong-grain 8.5 x 11" book. Judging from the sample books that I've received from various digital printers, only a small minority seem concerned about using correct-grain paper.

When all is said and done, I wind up back at my original statement: Digital books aren't necessarily bad, but they are different. Your best bet in ordering digital printing is to find an old-line book printer who made the move to digital printing rather than one who has always been a digital printer. Chances are the old-line printer is used to running books with correct-grain paper and binding books that don't fall apart. Chances are also good that he is running a true perfect binder, not the bargain basement version run by most digital shops. Most straight digital book printers lack the experience to know any better or the money to do anything about it. As a buyer you need to be clear in you mind as to what you are buying. The digital book printers used by *SelfPublishing.com* were all producing good books long before anyone ever heard the term POD (print on demand). If a printer is quoting for a run under about 750 copies, he is probably figuring to run on a digital press. Do yourself a favor when dealing with one of these printers and confirm that at least the paper grain to be used is correct. If the printer representative doesn't know what you are talking about or tells you that it doesn't matter, hang up the phone and try someone else.

Finally, no matter how much you want it to happen, you are not going to achieve A or even A– quality with digital printing. If that is what you require, you need to either raise your quantity to run at an offset printing plant or put your money back in your pocket and try again in few years or so.

Is white considered a color in printing?

No. The white of the paper never counts as a color. A one-color cover is one ink color on white paper, so unless you fill up the whole cover with that ink—it could be black or red or green or any other color—you'll have contrast. You start with blank cover stock and you add one ink to it, and you have a one-color cover. A two-color cover is two colors on white, and a three-color cover is three colors on white. Designers often use screens to get other tints or colors without having to pay for them. For example, a 50% screen used with black will yield a gray tint in the area screened, and a 50% screen of red will yield a pink tint, and so on. In addition, the combination of two screens gives the effect of a third color (blue plus yellow equals green, yellow plus red equals orange, and so forth). Once you get to four-color, the rules change.

Sometimes people new to publishing make the mistake of not thinking of black as a color. It surely is.

What trim size should I use?

Trim size relates to subject matter and perceived value. There are five basic trim sizes. The mass-market paperback size is 4.25 x 7". This size is associated with both fiction and nonfiction, and it represents the low end of the retail price range. Short-run methods do not efficiently produce books of this size. You need a press run of about 5,000 books to obtain a unit cost that works with a standard pricing formula.

The trade paperback size can be either 5.5 x 8.5" or 6 x 9". For quantities under 500, the actual trim size is closer to 5.25 x 8.25" due to short-run equipment limitations. (The actual trim size of this book is 5.25 x 8.25" because of this.) The 6 x 9" size does not work efficiently on most short-run processes. A standard DocuTech™ is limited to printing only four 6 x 9" pages at a time, versus eight pages at a time using a trim size of 5.25 x 8.25". The short-run offset presses use an 11 x 17" sheet and are subject to the same limitations. The longer-run presses are different. If you are running at least 500 copies, the 6 x 9" trim size costs only about 5% more than the 5.5 x 8.5". Trade paperback books carry a higher retail price than mass-market books. Trade paperbacks are also sometimes called "quality paperbacks." Generally, "quality" refers to the offset paper used.

The standard textbook size is 7 x 10". Many software manuals and cookbooks are also printed in this size.

The workbook size is 8.5 x 11". This size is standard for both short-run and long-run equipment. "How to" books and other nonfiction works fit this trim size well. You would never consider this size for a novel, however. For short runs, there's no price difference between this size and 7 x 10".

Should I be looking outside the United States to print my black-and-white book?

Generally the answer is no. Papers, plates, and ink—the main materials in the printing process—cost the same here as they do anywhere else in the world. Printing presses and related equipment cost the same no matter where you go and must be maintained the same way worldwide. In the United States, we actually pay less than foreign consumers for uncoated book paper because the paper mills are right here.

Many foreign countries do have an advantage in labor rates, but it is a small one. Let's say that the unit cost of a book is $4, and $3 of that represents the cost of materials. That leaves only $1 that can be discounted. If the foreign labor rate is one-fourth that of the United States, there is a savings of 75 cents per book; but the books still must be shipped. In the end, the total savings amounts to pennies, if that. When you factor in the time needed for your books to reach this country by boat, foreign printing looks even less attractive. The exception to this rule is Canada, where they have plenty of raw materials and a favorable exchange rate with the United States, and they can deliver books on a timely basis using regular ground shipping. Even with these apparent advantages, it is still generally less expensive to use U.S. printers. Ninety-nine percent of the books printed by, *SelfPublishing.com* are printed in the United States.

Why can't I just go to a local printer?

I believe a personal anecdote will best answer this question. Several years ago I produced a monthly ad-supported comedy magazine called the *Broadneck Baloney*. It was thirty-two 8.5 x 11" pages, printed in two colors on 50# offset paper, and the circulation was 10,000. Although I live in Maryland, I got the lowest price from a firm in Dover, Delaware, that used a huge web press to print all 32 pages at the same time. It took them less than two hours to strip, print, fold, and staple my publication. Of course, they were very busy, and I had to schedule my time on their press in advance if I wanted to meet my first-of-the-month publication date.

During this period, a local printer prepared my letterhead, business cards, and flyers. He also distributed about a hundred of my *Broadneck Baloney* copies to his other customers each month. He wanted to give me a price on the *Broadneck Baloney*. Without telling him the price I was getting in Dover, I said that he couldn't possibly beat it. He insisted. I said OK. Several days later he sent me a written bid. It stated that he would be so kind as to print 10,000 copies of *Broadneck Baloney* for a mere $8,260. I was paying $1,240 in Dover.

Yes, I could have just gone to my local printer to have my comedy magazine manufactured on his one-color press that printed two pages at a time—if it weren't for that $7,020 I'd be throwing out the window!

What is true of magazines in this regard is true of books. One advantage of working with *SelfPublishing.com* is that their experts will make certain that the printer with the right press for your specifications prints your book.

What paper is best for the text?

Paper makes up over 50% of the cost of the average printing job. The right paper choice for your book project can mean the difference between losing money and making a profit. Paper is sold like meat—by the pound. Simply put, heavier paper costs more. Let's compare 50# ("fifty-pound") and 60#. The 60# is 20% heavier than the 50#. Assuming text paper makes up 50% of the cost of your book (that percentage increases with quantity), then using 50# paper instead of 60# will cut 20% or more off your paper cost, and 10% or more off your total cost.

Use one of the standard papers most publishers use for their books. Stay away from paper salesmen with swatch books. His or her detailed discussion of a paper's opacity, color, finish, brightness, and groundwood content is usually not intended to save you money. Select one of the stocks offered by *SelfPublishing.com*; the samples in this book are:

- 50# white offset (512ppi)
- 50# natural offset (400ppi)
- 60# white offset (444ppi)
- 60# recycled offset (434ppi)
- 45# Alternative Offset (400ppi)

How will you choose? Price, look, and feel.

Would using 20# bond paper for my text save money?

Good question. The answer is no. Let me explain why. The poundage of text paper in the United States is determined by the weight of 500 sheets measuring 25 x 38". That measurement of area is called the basis size. Five hundred sheets of 50# text paper measuring 25 x 38" weigh 50 pounds. Five hundred sheets of 60# text paper measuring 25 x 38" weigh 60 pounds, and so on.

The weight of bond paper, used mostly in copy shops, is calculated using a different basis size—17 x 22". Five hundred sheets of 20# bond measuring 17 x 22" weigh 20 pounds. Five hundred sheets of 24# bond measuring 17 x 22" weigh 24 pounds, and so on. If you do the math to compare the two different systems of weight measurement, guess what? The 20# bond is the same as the 50# offset, and the 24# bond is the same as the 60# offset. Why two different basis sizes for text and bond paper were established, I don't know and no one can tell me. At least now it won't confuse you any more.

"I was an archaeologist before I became a self publisher."
"Really? What made you get out of archaeology?"
"My career was in ruins."

Does a heavier text paper mean a thicker book?

Not necessarily. Because of different manufacturing techniques, the weight of the paper and the number of pages
per inch (ppi) are not always proportional. The 50# white
offset suggested by *SelfPublishing.com* is 512 ppi, and the 60#
offset is 434 ppi. But if you look at the 50# natural offset, it
has almost the same ppi as the 60# white. If you're thinking
of printing your book on 60# offset for bulk, you could use
50# natural or 45# Alternative Offset and have almost the
same bulk.

Compare the different papers in this book and then use
the instant pricing feature on the *SelfPublishing.com* Web site
to make up your own mind.

What about the Alternative Offset and the recycled offset? When should I use these?

We have recently added two new papers and deleted one. The two new additions are 45# Alternative Offset and 60# Offset with 30% post-consumer recycled content. Both of these new sheets are around 400 ppi, so with the exception of our regular 50# white offset, which is 512 ppi, all of our text papers are now about the same thickness. The 45# Alternative Offset is much brighter than the old novel news due to chemical whitening. It is priced a little lower than the 50# offset and is a popular sheet with the larger publishers. The one downside of this sheet is that it will start to yellow sooner than the regular 50# offset due to the groundwood content. If you don't expect to sell out your press run in a year or less, I wouldn't recommend using it.

The 60# recycled offset, on the other hand, is significantly more expensive than the regular 60# offset because the larger publishers have been slow in increasing their demand for recycled paper, making it more expensive to produce. It looks more or less the same as the regular 60# offset. If ecology is number one on your list, this may be the paper stock for you. I suggest that you go *SelfPublishing.com* and try pricing your book in different ways. You will definitely be a trendsetter if you use the recycled paper, but you still need to make money to stay in business. Very few, if any, books command a higher retail price solely from being printed on recycled paper.

The 5 pt. novel news, which is the brown/gray paper you see in the mass-market paperback books in the drugstore, is still available in the mass-market size but only in quantities of 5,000 or greater.

What kind of cover paper should I use for my book?

I recommend what we have used for this book—10-point cover stock, coated on one side. It is measured not by weight, but by caliper (1 point is equal to 1/72"). That means if you stack up 1,000 sheets of 10-point cover stock, it will be about 10 inches high. What will its weight be? You can't determine that exactly, because different paper mills produce different densities of cover stock. Three stacks of 1,000 sheets of 10-point cover stock from three different paper mills will most likely have three different weights.

What are the different ways I can have my book printed?

Digital Printing

Because it is relatively new, digital printing gets a lot of attention these days. Digital is associated with on-demand printing, which is associated with short runs, low cost, and fast turnaround. Do most on-demand printers live up to the hype? Not really, but it's better than it was even a few years ago, and it's definitely here to stay.

Xerox® pioneered on-demand technology with its DocuTech™. If you've been to a printing or publishing trade show in the last several years, you've seen Team Xerox® producing perfect-bound and sometimes case-bound books in a slow, methodical way right before your eyes. Is this process fast for short runs of books? Sure it is. Is it less expensive than other forms of short-run printing? Until a few years ago, despite the hype, the answer was no. Now the answer is yes, depending on the company, equipment, and pricing philosophy. *SelfPublishing.com* originally used short-run offset for all quantities from 100 to 500 because it was less expensive than digital. That is no longer the case.

The path to the new "economies" of digital printing probably started with the entry of competition on the equipment side of the equation. Where Xerox® once enjoyed a near monopoly; there are now many newcomers to the field of digital printing. Increased competition on the equipment side has led to a general lowering of the cost of digital book printing. *SelfPublishing.com* uses printers who have a variety of digital equipment.

What are the strengths of digital printing? A digital press can take the digital files from your computer and go straight to print. In the case of text type, it's hard to tell the difference between the different types of equipment. The main difference comes in the reproduction of halftones (pictures). The Xerox® product looks like a "Xerox®" copy (because it is). While many people are getting used to the "toner" look, most still consider it an inferior product compared with offset printing. Some of the other digital presses do a somewhat better job on halftones, but if you want good halftones, order 500 or more copies of your book so that it can be printed on an offset press.

What is the major weakness of digital printing? There is no real quantity discount; your unit cost stays more or less the same no matter what quantity you print. That's great if you want a small number of copies but not so great if you want several thousand copies. Digital "printing" is generally more expensive than offset in quantities over 500.

Short-Run Offset

Short-run offset printing is a scaled-down version of the traditional book manufacturing process. The average short-run press prints 8 pages of a 5.5 x 8.5" book at a time, compared with 32, 64, or 128 pages at a time for the traditional sheetfed book press. While the traditional sheetfed press uses metal plates, the short-run press uses less expensive plates made directly from your digital files.

The finishing processes for digital and short-run offset are essentially the same. The sheets go to "little" collators, then to "little" perfect or case binders, and then to "little" cutters to complete the book. Short-run offset is real printing. Your book looks like a book, feels like a book, and smells like a book. The only real downsides are that the ink density from the front to the back of the sheet may vary a bit, and the press doesn't do the best job with halftones. The price for short-run offset is about 30% higher than digital printing on quantities of 100 and falls to only about 15% higher on quantities of 400 to 500. *SelfPublishing.com* uses this process only when specifically requested by the customer.

Traditional Sheetfed Printing

The traditional sheetfed press sees little use in today's book manufacturing. I can almost guarantee that if your book is being printed on a sheetfed offset press, you are paying more than you need to. This method used to fill the gap between short-run sheetfed and web presses. That is no longer true due to the fact that the newer web presses are efficient right down to around 500 copies, where the short-run presses leave off. There is still room for traditional sheetfed printing, however. Few web presses and hardly any digital presses can print on coated paper. A sheetfed press using metal plates on coated paper does a much better job on halftones than any other process. Using a standard paper and trim size, the traditional sheetfed press cannot compete with modern web presses. If you want coated glossy paper for a lot of halftones, and/or your book has an odd trim size, traditional sheetfed printing may be the best choice for you.

Web Offset

A web press prints using rolls of paper, which are cheaper than sheets; and at the end of the press run, it delivers a folded signature instead of a flat sheet, thus consolidating two book manufacturing processes. Running speeds sometimes exceed 25,000 impressions per hour. This compares with about 2,000 per hour on the short-run presses and about 5,000 per hour on the larger sheetfed presses.

The amount of makeready spoilage used to be very high on web presses, making them economical only for quantities over 5,000 or so. This has all changed for those printers who have replaced their decades-old webs with the more efficient up-to-date machinery. Modern-day makereadies are extremely efficient and spoilage is low. The advantages of a web press are speed and cost. If you are printing more than 500 copies of a standard-size book on uncoated paper, there are no disadvantages to printing on the web.

"How did you get into self publishing?"
"I decided to go into it after I lost my job because of something my boss said."
"What did he say?"
"You're fired."

How many books should I print?

Not counting books used for promotion, you shouldn't print a single book more than you can sell.

If your book size is 4.25 x 7", 5.5 x 8.5", 6 x 9", 7 x 10" or 8.5 x 11", you can get instant prices at *SelfPublishing.com*. Quantities for 5.5 x 8.5", 6 x 9", 7 x 10" and 8.5 x 11" start as low as a hundred. The mass-market size (4.25 x 7") starts at 1,000. You know what your budget is. Get prices on 100, 500, 1,000, or other appropriate amounts and think it through. The larger the quantity, the lower the unit cost. But what good is the lowest unit cost if most of the books stay stacked up in the garage?

When you are analyzing your unit cost, keep in mind that you will have to offer large distributors like *Amazon.com* a 60% discount off the retail price in order for them to sell your book.

Novelist: "I think I'll have my villain die after drinking a bucket of varnish."
Editor: "That's not such a bad finish."

What is four-color process?

A four-color cover is normally not four flat colors. The term "four-color" refers to the three process colors of yellow, cyan (blue), and magenta (red) plus black. From these four colors, printed in screens of dots, one on top of the other, you can make almost all the colors in the spectrum. Any time you see a "full-color" photograph printed in a book or magazine, it's four-color process. Any time a cover looks like it has more than two colors, it's probably a four-color cover. The next time you notice a blurry picture in a color newspaper, take a closer look and you'll see how the process works. The picture is blurry because the press was "out of register." Sometimes the register is so bad you can actually see the different-color dots.

Can I print color pictures in my book cost-effectively?

No. Although prepress costs have fallen dramatically in the last decade or so, four-color process printing is still expensive. Printing a full-color 16-page signature in a 5.5 x 8.5" book will cost you about $1,000 for film and proofs or $800 computer-to-plate, and another $1,000 or so for the plates and printing. If you're printing only 500 books, that's a unit cost of $4 per book just for the 16-page color signature. Using a standard markup of five or six times the production cost to figure your retail price, you would have to add an additional $24 per book to make the numbers work out profitably.

I have discussed my "Secrets of the Parthenon" series of books—all four-color throughout—with the experts at *SelfPublishing.com*. They estimate that I will have to print 20,000 copies of each book in order to get my unit cost low enough to set a retail price under $20. These are very specialized books that wouldn't make sense to print in black and white. I need some investors.

So, unless you have a special case as I do, using color in the body of your book is not a good idea. The exception to this is children's picture books.

What is perfect binding, and should I use it for my book?

Perfect binding is also called adhesive binding or softback binding. There are also some patented processes such as Lay-Flat™ and Ota-Bind™. These processes gather pages together in a stack, grind off one-eighth of an inch of the backbone, rough it up, and apply adhesive. Then the machinery applies the paper cover to the glued book block, squares it off, and trims the three other sides to make the final book.

Perfect binding is the least expensive form of book-binding, and most self publishers use it. The perfect binding process is efficient down to as few as 100 copies. Perfect binding creates a flat spine where the title, author, and publisher are printed. Stores like this because they can display the book spine out, saving them valuable shelf space. The downside is that libraries generally prefer to buy hard-cover books.

What about saddle stitching?

Saddle stitching is less expensive for books of 64 pages or less. Instead of piling the signatures on top of each other, as with perfect binding, signatures are wrapped around each other on a "saddle," wire-stitched, and then trimmed on three sides. This binding is great if you're producing a newsletter for the local PTA—but not if you're trying to sell a book. Saddle stitching has a much lower perceived value. Since they do not have a spine and thus would have to be displayed face out, bookstores do not want saddle-stitched books. The exceptions to this rule are certain types of children's picture books.

How about hardcover binding?

Hardcover or case binding is certainly the top-of-the-line type of binding. It is accepted by all retail outlets and libraries and has a much higher perceived value. It is also the most expensive style of binding, especially in low quantities, so it presents a financial roadblock to most self publishers. Within the hardcover category there are many options such as sewing versus adhesive, cloth versus paper, stamping, and a casewrap and/or a printed jacket. In the spirit of "tires off the rack," *SelfPublishing.com* has come up with a standard set of hardcover specifications that gives the self publisher an affordable option. For 100 to 400 copies they offer an unjacketed book, but it does have a digitally printed casewrap (see page 59 if this term is unfamiliar to you). For quantities of 500 and more, *SelfPublishing.com* offers standard imitation cloth, stamped on the spine with or without a printed jacket.

What about all those "terms and conditions"?

Terms and conditions are important. They lay out the basic ground rules governing the printing industry. Printing customs are the commonsense guidelines within which the printing industry works. If you believe in treating others the way you would like to be treated yourself, then you'll be fine, and the subject of printing customs won't even come up. Generally, printers are quite fair and will try to do everything within their power to make you, the customer, happy. If you act unfairly or make unrealistic demands, that's when printers are forced to stick strictly to the terms and conditions.

Let me give you a personal experience that may bring the point home. The third issue of my magazine *Broadneck Hundred* looked great. The editorial content, the photographs, and the cover were better than anything that I, or the competition, had produced. It cost a lot of money to reach that level of excellence, and I didn't have enough money left to pay the printer. Because I had produced such a "remarkable" publication, I expected the printer to release the magazines to me and let me pay for them as I sold them. Of course, the printer refused. At eight o'clock the next morning I and some associates tried to carry as many boxes of magazines out the back door of the printing plant as we could. The police stopped us. Oops! Those were not my magazines, and they wouldn't be mine until I paid for them. We were stealing.

I came to my senses, apologized to the printer, and borrowed the money to pay him. I have to chalk that one up to egotism and immaturity. I had confused the printer with the bank, and imagined that my upstart pretensions entitled me to special privileges. I had violated printing customs, but you wouldn't have had to read them to know that I was in the wrong.

I think it's basically this simple: If the printer produces commercially acceptable books that you ordered, you must pay for them.

You have an opportunity to read the Printing Trade Customs in the Production Center of *SelfPublishing.com*.

Do I have to pay for the extra books if there is an overrun?

Yes, you do have to pay for overruns up to 10% of your ordered quantity. If, for example, you order 2,000 books, and 2,100 or 2,200 books are shipped, you must pay for the extra 100 or 200 books. The reason is that printers cannot estimate spoilage in the printing process exactly. According to custom, a 10% overrun or a 10% underrun counts as a complete job. You get charged for an overrun and credited for an underrun. (In other words, if you order 2,000 books and receive 1,800 books, your order is considered complete.) If you absolutely must have a minimum quantity, then the spoilage factor doubles to 20% on the plus side. If your minimum is 2,000 books, for example, then you must accept an overrun of up to 2,400. *SelfPublishing.com* does its best to hold its printers to a 5% variability, and generally orders done digitally yield the exact number ordered.

Why don't cannibals eat self publishers?
Because they know that you can't keep a good person down.

Can I get a discount on the printing bill if my books arrive late?

No—unless you have a written guarantee of a specific date spelling out the conditions and/or consequences if that date is not met. Book printers have a general idea how long it takes to print a book in their plant. The actual time it takes depends more often on you. How well is your book prepared? How long will you hold the proofs? How many changes will you make?

SelfPublishing.com strives for realistic and consistent delivery dates. The roots of its parent company, RJ Communications, are in commercial printing, where the schedules are very tight, being geared toward trade shows and other dated events; thus they have an excellent track record for meeting deadlines. To be on the safe side, however, don't plan your publication party or schedule a book signing until you have the books in hand. Remember, even if you are told Monday that your books will ship on Friday, lots of unforeseen things can happen.

Writer: "Last night I dreamt I was a vice."
Editor: "For God's sake, get a grip on yourself."

Can I make corrections to my proofs?

Yes, you can make corrections to your proofs. Keep in mind that if they are editorial changes ("author's alterations"), there will be fees involved. If the errors you find involve formatting issues, the question of responsibility becomes a bit grayer. What is definitely not "gray" is that once you OK a proof, and if the printed book matches the proof, you own those copies. So check your proofs carefully, because—trust me—I have seen a lot of funky things happen at the proof stage.

The printer damaged my disc; what can I do?

If you didn't keep a copy, not much—cry maybe. It is very important that you keep copies of anything you send to the printer. This includes all text files and digital images. There are true horror stories about writers who spent years on their manuscripts, and then, not having a copy, lost them somehow. Don't take a chance; cover yourself every step of the way with copies of your work.

What about shipping costs?

Unless it is otherwise stated, you pay the shipping costs from the printer to the destination you specify. On smaller runs shipping is generally done by UPS. Shipping costs are a little like author's alterations in that nobody is happy with the costs, nobody makes any money on it, and it can be a source of contention if the cost comes as a surprise at the end. As you're pacing around waiting for your books after approving the proofs, do yourself a favor and research the best way to ship your books. Remember, printers are printers. They might have shipping departments, but they are not in the shipping business. The printer can suggest the best way to ship your books, but the money for it is coming out of your pocket. The money you save on shipping costs translates into a few less books you will have to sell to break even.

Generally, books are shipped in 35-pound cartons. You can estimate how much your books weigh by asking the printer or by taking a book with similar dimensions and paper off your bookshelf and weighing it. Then calculate how many books there are per carton to figure out how many cartons you'll have. You can then go to *UPS.com* and get the actual cost of the shipping or a very close approximation. All you need is the printer's zip code and the zip code where you want the books sent, and you're in business.

Quantities over 1,000 copies are generally better shipped LTL (less than truckload) via common carrier. *Freightquote.com* is a Web site that lets you compare the costs of various carriers to almost anywhere in the country.

When my book sells out, does a reprint cost less than the first printing?

No, and the reason is that because we are using direct-to-plate technology with your PDF files, we do all of the same steps all over again. You may be able to skip a proof review, though, and that could save you a bit of time, but there are no monetary savings for reprinting.

For details on the printing process, see pages 84-87. Actual paper shade may vary from printer to printer. The same images on these pages appear in other sections of the book for comparison.

Helvetica thin	12 on 18 leading	15% black background
Helvetica thin	12 on 18 leading	no background
Helvetica	12 on 18 leading	30% black background
Helvetica	12 on 18 leading	no background
Helvetica medium	12 on 18 leading	60% black background
Helvetica medium	12 on 18 leading	no background
Helvetica black	12 on 18 leading	75% black background
Helvetica black	12 on 18 leading	no background
Helvetica black	12 on 18 leading	100% black background

Chapter 23

Chapter 24

IMAGE SECTION

MARKETING QUESTIONS

Should I try to get a trade book distributor?

I would at least try to get a distributor for your book. Note: I said "try." Don't get discouraged if you initially come up empty on this one. A distributor will take a 60–75% discount off the retail price to get your book placed in the various wholesale and retail databases so that it is available to the bookstore buyers. Many small publishers put way too much emphasis on this part of the process. Getting a distributor does not guarantee you any actual sales. It does make it easier, however, when you get enough publicity to create a demand for your book. A true distributor works on a commission based on the total sales of the book. In other words, the distributor is not making money unless you are. Beware of those who say they want to distribute your book but want you to pay $500–1,500 to get you "set up."

My personal favorite is Biblio Distributors. They were established for the sole purpose of distributing books for the small press publisher. Their startup fee is low, and their monthly storage rates are quite reasonable. They are not interested in books printed digitally so you'll probably need to print at least 500 copies. They are also not interested in your book if you are not the ISBN owner (and if you are still considering letting someone assign you one of their ISBNs at this stage, you should see a psychiatrist.) Whatever you do in the way of hiring a distributor, remember that the distributor will only make your book available to the right places. It's up to you to get the right places to want your book.

What can I do to qualify to be distributed by Biblio or any other trade distributor?

The Biblio review committee accepts only about 10–15% of the submissions they receive; the rest are sent a letter and an evaluation form explaining why Biblio decided not to offer a contract. Overall their goal is to offer contracts only to small presses that they feel publish books they can sell through retail and online bookstores.

Here are Biblio's primary reasons for declining a book:

Market: The trade market is very competitive, and they feel that your publishing company is not quite ready or that the market is flooded with similar titles. *Note:* Fiction, poetry, business and economics, self-help, and children's books are particularly hard to sell in the trade market because these categories are so heavily published.

Not right for the trade market: Your title may be better suited for special sales, or the academic and library market. You might consider selling through religious bookstores, direct mail, lectures and seminars, regional bookstores, and online retailers to best reach your audience. You might consider working with a library and/or academic distributor.

Basic book requirements not met (e.g., no ISBN, no bar code, no price on book, price too high, price too low): The price on your book must be competitive for your category, page count, and format. The major accounts are very price-sensitive and the competition is fierce.

Marketing and promotion: The book does not appear to be supported via advertising, marketing, or promotion. Books do not sell just by being on the bookstore shelf or through "word of mouth" alone. They must have a solid promotion planned in advance of any sales efforts or publication. In addition, Web-based promotion is rarely effective for the trade market. Special sales or back-of-the-room sales do not influence the trade market.

Design: The production value of your book is not competitive with other books in the category. With the vast quantity of books published every year, packaging is the key to sales. Design elements include the typeface, jacket, layout, photo reproduction, table of contents, index, and other features. A spine with the title is essential for placement on store shelves.

Limited subject matter (e.g., poetry or the self publisher's memoir). Poetry and personal memoirs are very difficult for Biblio to sell. The audience is extremely limited. Your best options are online retailers and your local bookstore.

Rights/publisher: The applicant is not the owner of the book or ISBN prefix; Xlibris, Lightning Source, or some other such organization is the publisher. Publishers must apply for distribution, not authors.

Future publishing plans: There is no indication of future publishing plans, and the title submitted is not strong enough on its own to support full distribution efforts. *Or* future plans are not focused enough to build a program upon; the publisher should choose a niche market on which to focus its efforts.

Appears to be POD: Biblio does not accept print-on-demand books at this time because their customers will not carry POD books. If you decide to go to offset printing, please feel free to resubmit.

Publishers are encouraged to resubmit their titles when they have addressed Biblio's concerns and are ready to try again. If you need professional help in any of these areas, contact one of the companies listed at Biblio's Web site, *bibliodistribution.com/publishers/resources*.

For additional information refer to the Publishing Basics Radio interview with Davida Breier, sales and marketing manager of Biblio, which is posted in the Past Shows section of *wbjbradio.com*.

What can I do if I can't find a distributor, like Biblio, to distribute my book to the trade?

Most of you decided to self publish because your manuscript was rejected by one, two, five, or one hundred traditional publishers. Being rejected by a distributor at this point is no big deal. After a moment or two of silence, you should head full speed into Plan B. Remember earlier in the book when we talked about POD (print on demand)? How about the final reason listed above for Biblio's rejecting a book for distribution? Now that we have told you everything bad about POD, let me tell you one good thing about it. Back in the early 1990s Ingram Book Group, one of the world's largest book wholesalers, announced that they were no longer dealing directly with small publishers. If a small publisher wanted to be carried by Ingram, they either needed to be picked up by a distributor (like Biblio) or use the POD printing company Ingram owned, Lightning Source. Lightning Source is one of the very few true POD (one at a time) printers in the country. They can afford to be a one-at-a-time printer because their plant is three blocks away from Ingram's main warehouse, making shipping minimal. Lightning Source is tied into a distribution network that includes Ingram, Baker & Taylor, Amazon, and Barnes & Noble. Here's how it works: In the case of a book ordered on Amazon, the consumer places the order at Amazon. The order is then sent electronically to Lightning Source, which prints and ships the books within 24 hours. The publisher is then paid the difference between the wholesale price and the cost of the POD printing. Pretty neat, huh?

In an effort to make something good even better, RJ Communications, the owner of *SelfPublishing.com*, made a deal with Lightning Source to offer their service at a discount to *SelfPublishing.com* customers—thus the creation of their exclusive Thor Distribution program. The advantage of using the Thor program rather than working with Lightning Source directly is threefold. First, the startup costs are less: $49.95 for Thor versus $100 plus an initial fee for Lightning Source. Second, you get your money quicker. Lightning Source pays publishers 90 days after the end of the month of the sale. Thor pays publishers quarterly on all sales made during the previous quarter. (So for a book sold on March 2 Lightning Source pays the publisher on July 1. With Thor, the publisher would be paid on April 15.) Third, and perhaps most important, Thor looks at POD distribution as a program that is meant to be outgrown as soon as possible. It is an easy, inexpensive way to get your book listed in all the book wholesalers' and retailers' databases so that it will be available at pretty much every store in the country. Please note that I said "available." There is a huge difference between a book being on the bookshelf (for example, through Biblio) and a book being available for order, but it's a start. It will give you time to establish the market that was possibly missing the first time you presented your book to a distributor. In my interview with Davida Breier from Biblio, she reinforced the idea that Thor is the perfect alternative to traditional distribution and has no problem picking up a book once the publisher can prove that demand for the title exists based on the POD sales.

If I use the Thor POD distribution system, why do I also need to buy a regular press run of books?

The answer to this is simple. First off, even on a good day, only about 25% of the total books you sell will be to bookstores; the other 75% will be sold to alternative markets. It is these alternative markets where the author/publisher has the best chance of being successful through his or her own efforts. Real books are needed for this. You also need real books for promotion and to send out for review. Also, you will most likely need printed books if you are going to do any in-store book signings. Bookstores don't normally want to order non-returnable books, which is the form in which POD books are sold. In short, POD distribution is merely a starting point. It is not as good as being carried by a traditional distributor, but it is infinitely better than having no outlet at all.

In what other ways do you suggest I market my book?

Technically, this should probably be one of the first questions in this book. It is certainly as important as any question, perhaps second only to "Do I need my own ISBN?" This section is intended not to replace other book marketing information that is available from a variety of sources, only supplement it.

You do not want to start with an order from Barnes & Noble for 30,000 copies

As much as you might believe the contrary, the last thing you want is a nice, fat, 30,000-copy book order from Barnes & Noble. Bookstores buy books that are 100% returnable. Unfortunately, B&N does not care that you just took another mortgage on your house to pay for the printing of 30,000 copies of your book based on their purchase order. There is absolutely nothing stopping them from returning 28,000 of these books several months later, filling your garage with books and leaving you with 180 or 360 easy payments on your new mortgage. Don't worry, there is plenty of time for Barnes & Noble. Once there is enough demand, you can sell your book to them non-returnable. If not B&N, what then?

1001 Ways to Market Your Book

The first thing you need to do is visit *JustBookz.com* and buy a discounted copy of John Kremer's *1001 Ways to Market Your Book*. It's been around for a while and some of the statistical data is a little dated, but you can't go wrong picking up a copy. I guarantee you will pick up a few tips that will be more than worth your while and help you sell books.

Press Release

A good press release is a little like a good cover design. The *SelfPublishing.com* people lean toward the lower-priced, higher-quality companies. *SelfPublishing.com* works closely with an agency located at *Send2Press.com*. There are a wide range of services available. The one thing I would highly recommend is to have them edit your press release or even write it for you. It's an affordable expense that will significantly increase the odds of getting people in the media to react to your release. Be realistic, though, in what you expect from a press release. For the most part, reporters aren't sitting there just waiting for you to come along so that they can interview you and give you free publicity. One good by-product of sending out a press release is that even if you do not get any calls from the press, your press release will appear on hundreds of Web sites all over the Internet. Make sure you have your Web site linked to your press release. You never know who will click through and take a look

JustBookz.com Online Bookstore

Started in late 2002, the *JustBookz.com* online bookstore was created to provide an affordable alternative to *Amazon.com* and *Barnes&Noble.com*. All *SelfPublishing.com* customers are eligible to be included in the store. There are no setup fees, and they charge only 25% of the retail price on sales, compared with the 55% charged by Amazon and B&N. Internet keyword marketing is also performed, at no cost to the author/publisher, if the book lends itself to this type of marketing. The theme of this bookstore is that Tom Clancy doesn't need any more of your money. Buy independent.

Create a Web Site

By 2006 this should be a no-brainer. Having a Web site gives you access to tens of millions of Internet users. There is no need to spend a lot of money setting up a site, although it needs to be professionally designed to be effective. If you are printing with *SelfPublishing.com*, there are many affordable options available starting at $9.96 per month. Web site design has its own subdomain at *SelfPublishing.com*. Click on the Web site's Design & Hosting tab at the top of the home page to find out which option best fits your needs.

Web Site Marketing

Now that you have a Web site with its own URL, it's time to get the word out to the masses. For around $100 you can have the people at *SelfPublishing.com*, or someone else, list your site with several thousand search engines. There is no magic involved. It's just a software program. It's pretty good. You'll get hundreds of emails from the various sites that will have you "feeling good" about your site in no time. You will certainly get your money's worth. There are a handful of "must" search engines to which your site needs to be submitted by hand. That shouldn't cost you more than another $25.

One of the most effective ways to have your book pop up to the top of the search engine listings is to sign up for one of the various "pay per click" engines. Simply put, you bid against other Web sites to have your site top-listed for various keywords. The easy terms are too expensive to make sense. For example, enter the word "self publishing" at Yahoo. The top four sites are paying over $7 per click for every visitor who clicks on their listing. Want to have some fun? Go to Yahoo and enter the search term "self publishing" and visit the top five listings. Guess what types of services are willing to pay that much to get you to visit them? Be creative. You do not need to spend more than 10 or 15 cents per click for quality traffic. The good thing with these pay engines is that you can set your own limit and you pay only if the person actually visits your site.

Special-Sales Marketing

My friend Brian Jud, a well-known marketing guru for small press publishers, has developed several tools to help guide you to non-bookstore markets in which to sell your book.

First is the Special-Sales Profit Center™, a Web-based, prospect-rich, targeted marketing system that helps deliver incremental sales and profits to you. The Profit Center is an online contact management system that gives you a continuing supply of sales leads customized for each of your titles. It can increase your productivity by organizing the process of contacting prospects and converting them to customers. The Profit Center can improve your profitability by directing your sales efforts to those most likely to buy your titles. Since it is Web-based, it permits access from remote locations so you can have the information you need wherever you are.

Second is Brian's book *Beyond the Bookstore,* a Publishers Weekly selection that shows you how to sell your books to non-bookstore markets, more profitably with no returns. There are seventy-nine strategies in *Beyond the Bookstore* that show you how to tap the enormous, lucrative market of special sales. You will discover the secrets of selling more of your books in new places, increasing sales and profits as you reduce returns, and contacting buyers successfully.

Beyond the Bookstore contains the *Marketing Planning* CD-ROM™, with templates for planning and tracking sales and expenses. This CD-ROM walks you through the steps for creating a customized marketing plan. It helps you increase profits by offering practical marketing help. For more information, see Step 4, Marketing and Distribution, at *SelfPublishing.com*.

Learn to Expertize

Another thing I'd highly recommend you do, if you want more attention for your book from major magazines, newspapers, and talk shows, is learn something about Fern Reiss's *Expertizing*. Fern has been quoted, and her books mentioned, in over 100 publications, from the New York Times and the Wall Street Journal to Fortune Small Business and Wall Street Week to USA Today and Glamour Magazine. *Expertizing* is about getting more media attention for your book and business, and Fern has *Expertized* small businesses, large businesses, and nonprofits—everyone from the Hilton Hotels Corporation to the United Methodist Church. Most of her *Expertizing* techniques work particularly well for authors and independent publishers.

One example of what you'll learn in *Expertizing* is how to generate irresistible media soundbites. A few years back, Fern wanted to get some media attention for her book, "Terrorism and Kids: Comforting Your Child." She noticed that a Voice of America reporter was doing a story, and since Voice of America broadcasts to an international audience, thought it might be a good way to get foreign sales. The problem was, the journalist wasn't doing a piece on terrorism. He was doing a story on the sudden popularity of home theatre systems. But Fern managed to get an astounding 15 minutes on Voice of America, in his piece on home theatre systems, for her book on "Terrorism and Kids." Here's what she emailed the journalist:

> "You can thank Osama bin Laden for the sudden popularity of home theatre systems. Americans, post 9/11, are bringing their entertainment into their homes; it's a 9/11 nesting response. And I'm the author of a book, "Terrorism and Kids: Comforting Your Child..." Once you learn this sort of technique, you can get into any publication—with any book—on any topic!
>
> Fern's all day *Expertizing* workshops happen at the Ritz Carlton Hotels in Boston, New York, and San Francisco, or you can sign up for her free monthly *Expertizing* email newsletter. For more information see Step 4, Marketing and Distribution at *SelfPublishing.com*.

Online Radio Showcases

I started a Podcast, which is a fancy word for online radio show, during the summer of 2005. My show is titled Publishing Basics Radio, where weekly we help you navigate the self publishing minefield. Audio on the Internet is something that I have toyed with for the past couple years. The availability of cable and DSL connections affordable to just about anyone, in combination with the explosion of Apple's iPod, has made online audio a reality. Errol Smith, a pioneer of the Readers Radio Network, and Allan Hunkin, the owner of *Podcast.com*, are two of the leaders in this field, and both have programs of special interest to publishers.

Readers Radio has a network of over 10,000 Web sites that have agreed to sell books within the site's particular specialty. With Readers Radio, you are interviewed by Emmy award winner Errol Smith about your book. This interview is edited and then posted on sites within the Readers Radio Network as well as sites researched by the author. For this service Readers Radio is paid a reasonable fee plus a percentage of the sales of all books sold though the network. Allan Hunkin has a similar program, where the author is interviewed, for a reasonable fee, and then is given the interview outright to use in marketing his or her books. Both programs are good and affordable. You can find out more information about these programs at *SelfPublishing.com*.

Trade Shows

Trade shows are a good way of getting your book in front of many retail book buyers. Unfortunately, they are quite expensive for a one- or two-book publisher and are rarely the "pot of gold at the end of the rainbow" that all newcomers envision to be. Your best bet is to ease into these shows. The largest show in the United States is the annual Book Expo America. This show generally moves between New York, Chicago, and Los Angeles, although the 2006 show is in Washington DC. The least expensive way to participate in this as well as many regional shows is to join Publishers Marketing Association (PMA) and take part in one of their co-op programs.

Trade Associations

I purposely left trade associations for last. There are many different trade associations that cater to the small press customer. Unfortunately, very few (if any) of these organizations want a press that is too small (like you, with your single title). They will all let you join and have nice newsletters, but keep in mind that most of the information they provide and the services they offer are really meant for the larger independent publisher. Personally, I feel that there is a need for a trade association specifically geared to the one- and two-title publisher. After your third or fourth title, you graduate to one of the other associations. Maybe RJ Communications will start such an association one day. For now you're on your own. The two main small press associations are PMA and SPAN (Small Press Association of North America).

Remember, your book is not going to sell itself. The only way that there will be demand for your book is if you help create that demand. Luck replaces hard work only in very rare circumstances.

Are there ways to be sure I make money on my book?

I believe you can find ways if you put your mind to it. I have been fortunate enough to do so with one of my self published books, *Soups and Stories from the Realm of Queen Arnold*. Dick Elms, a retired printer and proofreader, and a neighbor of mine, had fifty fabulous soup recipes he wanted to publish. That didn't seem to be enough for a book. As Penrod Waterman, I had published eight short stories over the years, but that was not enough to carry a book either. So we invented the great queen and her mythical realm.

Queen Arnold, as it turns out, arrived on Broadneck (a peninsula just north of Annapolis, Maryland, on Chesapeake Bay) from England on the seventh day of the seventh month of the 777th year with her party of 777 men, women, and children. Known for her enthralling sensual magnetism, her exuberant mirth, her extraordinary vivacity, her flawless beauty, her blunt rusticity, and her kiss-provoking lips, Queen Arnold ruled over an ideal realm for seventy-seven years. Back then, the Arnoldites ate soup just before darkness oozed around the forest; then, as delicately emerging stars and small campfires magnified the subduing charm of the woods, peerless raconteurs began to amuse and enchant young and old alike with fabulous stories.

I made sure the book made money by pre-selling 800 copies. In exchange for suggesting their wines as appropriate accompaniments to each of the fifty soup recipes, a group of affiliated wineries bought 400 of the books at just below the retail price. We dedicated the book to the memory of a great soup-making grandmother whose family still owned a local wine and spirits shop. They bought 200 copies to sell in their store. Then, in the acknowledgments, we touted a local tree service as being the most environmentally concerned and historically sensitive in the world. They bought 200 copies from us to give to their preferred customers in the Arnold area.

Not every book lends itself to these kinds of sales, but perhaps this example will inspire you to think of some pre-publication connections you can make.

How do I get my books made available from Amazon or Barnes & Noble?

The easiest way to get into either of these Web sites is to join *SelfPublishing.com*'s Thor distribution program. This POD program is a great entry-level form of distribution. For a small fee plus an equally small annual fee, your book will be listed in the Ingram database as well as Baker & Taylor, *Amazon.com*, *BarnesandNoble.com*, and the databases of over 25,000 nationwide bookstores. This is the same program sold by virtually all of the POD publishers as their sole means of distribution. It is no good as a sole means of distribution, but is the perfect supplement to traditional book selling. You can check out more on this in the Distribution section of *SelfPublishing.com*.

Will I be able to get my book on Oprah?

It's possible, but there are five conditions. First, you have to catch a weasel when it's asleep. Second, you have to make a silk purse out of a pig's ear. Third, you must extract sunbeams from cucumbers. Fourth, Elvis Presley must receive a posthumous best actor award for his portrayal of Jess Wade in *Charro*. And fifth, Mongolia must become the fifty-first state.

The point: Stay realistic. Work hard at marketing day by day. Wasn't it Edison who said, "Success is 1% inspiration and 99% perspiration"?

Index

Image section:
Printed digitally on 60# recycled offset, 434ppi.

For details on the printing process, see pages 84-87. Actual paper shade may vary from printer to printer. The same images on these pages appear in other sections of the book for comparison.

Helvetica thin	12 on 18 leading	15% black background
Helvetica thin	12 on 18 leading	no background
Helvetica	12 on 18 leading	30% black background
Helvetica	12 on 18 leading	no background
Helvetica medium	12 on 18 leading	60% black background
Helvetica medium	**12 on 18 leading**	**no background**
Helvetica black	**12 on 18 leading**	**75% black background**
Helvetica black	**12 on 18 leading**	**no background**
Helvetica black	**12 on 18 leading**	**100% black background**

Chapter 23

Chapter 24

Image section:
Printed digitally on 60# white offset, 444ppi.

For details on the printing process, see pages 84-87. Actual paper shade may vary from printer to printer. The same images on these pages appear in other sections of the book for comparison.

Helvetica thin	12 on 18 leading	15% black background
Helvetica thin	12 on 18 leading	no background
Helvetica	12 on 18 leading	30% black background
Helvetica	12 on 18 leading	no background
Helvetica medium	12 on 18 leading	60% black background
Helvetica medium	**12 on 18 leading**	**no background**
Helvetica black	**12 on 18 leading**	**75% black background**
Helvetica black	**12 on 18 leading**	**no background**
Helvetica black	**12 on 18 leading**	**100% black background**

Chapter 23

Chapter 24